APPEARANCES

APPEARANCES

GIANNI CELATI
Translated by Stuart Hood

The publishers thank Kathy Acker, Mark Ainley, Martin Chalmers, John Kraniauskas, Mike Hart, Bob Lumley, Enrico Palandri, Kate Pullinger, for their editorial advice and assistance

Library of Congress Catalog Card Number:
90–64194

British Library Cataloguing in Publication Data
Celati. Gianni 1937–
Appearances.
I. Title   II. (Quattro novelle sulle apparenze) English
853.914(F)

ISBN 1–85242–212–2

First published as *Quattro novelle sulle apparenze* by
Feltrinelli Editore, Milan
Copyright © 1987 Giangiacomo Feltrinelli Editore, Milano
Translation © 1991 by Serpent's Tail

This edition first published 1991
by Serpent's Tail, 4 Blackstock Mews, London N4

Typeset in 10/12 pt Raleigh by Selectmove, London

Printed on acid-free paper by
Nørhaven A/S, Viborg, Denmark

Contents

BARATTO

I shall tell the story of how Baratto, coming home one evening, was bereft of thoughts, and then of the consequences of his living as a mute for a long time.

One Sunday towards the end of March, Baratto is playing a rugby match with his team. In the first half he makes a couple of breakaway moves and both times stops at the three-quarter line, shaking his head. His team's forwards did make a run in time to take his passes, and both times the ball was lost. He feels the match has nothing to do with him, he says so to a player with a stye on his eye who is playing with him in defence.

For a long time in mid-field there are only scrums followed by whistles from the referee, arguments between the players, arguments between the referee and the players, and shouts from the trainer on the bench. In the meantime Baratto walks up and down the touchline looking at the ground. At a certain point he shakes his head, then begins to abuse his comrades because they are arguing too much with the referee. Crossing the pitch, he shouts several times, 'There's nothing to argue about!' and abuses the referee as well because he doesn't blow his whistle to penalise them all.

One of his team mates — a huge man with a little head — runs over to clap him on the shoulder to calm him, 'Keep calm, Baratto,' he says, 'because things are going badly here.' For many months their team has always been losing and is bottom of the league.

Baratto shakes his head and replies: 'There's nothing to argue about. We've always been useless so it's right that we lose.'

When the other player — the one with the stye on his eye — comes up to hear what has happened Baratto explains it to him like this: 'I have broken my meniscus twice playing for you and what for?' Then he turns and goes off towards the dressing rooms. And when someone shouts to him: 'Baratto, where are you going then?' he, without stopping, replies that he doesn't feel like playing any more.

In the dressing rooms the trainer soon arrives with his cigar (which has gone out) in his mouth, trying to convince him to go back on to the pitch. He says everything is going to the dogs and he can't abandon a match like this: he is one of the best players on the field, the directors will want an explanation and what explanation can he (the trainer) give? While the other is talking to convince him, Baratto has stripped off.

The trainer still waits for an answer, he lights his cigar nervously and asks: 'Well then?' Baratto points to the cigar and gives him this answer: 'You smoke and you'll get cancer.' Then he sits on a little bench and shuts his eyes, announcing to the trainer that now he no longer wishes to talk to him.

With eyes shut, he begins to hold his breath and, after a few seconds, feels he can stay without breathing as long as he likes, without waiting for anything else, and without even the thought of being there. Later he loses his balance and falls from the little bench, finding himself on the ground.

On the way back to Piacenza on his motorbike he hasn't put his helmet on because his head is hot. On the road there are long lines of cars coming back after the Sunday drive in the country; he overtakes them on the hard shoulder looking round and observing the landscape.

It looks to him as if in the landscape there were smoke or steam and he keeps on thinking a sentence: 'There's smoke in this landscape.' So he stops on the edge of the road to have a better look and afterwards notices he isn't thinking that sentence any more, because the air is clear and cultivated fields can be seen to the horizon. On a little rise in the ground there are three isolated shadowless trees.

Before entering town he is stopped by the traffic police, a policeman signals to him from the edge of the road to point out that he isn't wearing a helmet. He stops and explains: 'My head is hot — my blood pressure must have gone up.' Then he turns round to look once again at the landscape in the distance, searching for the three isolated shadowless trees. He shuts his eyes and holds his breath, waiting until the young policeman comes and gives him back his documents telling him to put on his helmet. The policeman waves his disc as if he had no time to lose and immediately turns away to listen to another policeman. Baratto sets off again without putting on his helmet.

Coming back home he meets an old pensioner who lives on the floor below and who is watering a pot of azaleas on the landing. Bent over the pot the pensioner addresses him: 'The days are getting longer.' Baratto replies as he passes him: 'I can't answer now,' then goes into the house, slipping off his jacket which he lets fall on the floor.

The table in the living room is set, his wife sets it every day before going out. Lately his wife has been coming back late in the evening and maybe has another man, but Baratto hasn't asked her because it doesn't interest him. Every evening he prepares the food and eats standing in the little kitchen, and before going to bed clears the table so that his wife won't think something odd has happened. Coming back home when he is already in bed, his wife often has the leftovers also eating standing in the little kitchen; next day before going out she sets the table again for supper.

He has made himself a sandwich and eats it standing up examining his collection of foreign cigarette boxes. Some of the boxes are metal and he drums on them with his finger as he finishes chewing. He has turned on the television to an empty channel and stands there, looking at it and listening to its hum.

Meantime his head has got hot again. Then he takes a fan in the shape of a spatula and begins to fan his head.

Gradually as he fans himself there come into his mind phrases from commercials which he often hears on television. He walks to and fro in the room fanning himself and listening to the jingles which come to his mind. When he notices that they don't come to him any more he shakes his head slightly perplexed, then turns off the television and decides to go to bed.

As every evening, in the little kitchen he pours water round the edge of the sink where there are ants that come in through the window in long lines. In the bathroom he cleans his teeth and as he comes out of the bathroom seems to remember something, perhaps the caption under a picture in a magazine, but nothing precise.

Climbing the spiral stair that leads into the bedroom he takes off his shirt; in the bedroom he takes off all his clothes. And seeing himself there big and tall in the mirror of the wardrobe the thought comes to him: 'What could I think of now?' He stands swaying in front of the mirror but no sentence comes to mind.

On the ironing board there is a little electric alarm clock and Baratto watches the jerks of the second hand without understanding what they are trying to tell him personally. He stands there wondering a little, still swaying, but no idea comes into his mind. Then he takes his penis in his hand and thinks: 'I have no thoughts any more.'

He falls asleep almost at once face down on the bed and arms spread. After that he did not talk for many months and little by little his recovery began.

Baratto's wife filters telephone calls from morning to evening in an electronic toy factory, and says that in that factory they think she's a piece of electronic equipment too. This she gathers from the way they — directors of the firm and clients — talk to her. During the day too many things always happen that fill her head and stay in her head without going away, so to come home in the evening doesn't even feel like a relief to her. She is happy if an admirer comes by car to pick her up at the factory to take her for supper and makes advances towards her, because at least listening to advances gives her a certain happiness.

One evening Marta came home earlier than usual and found Baratto in the little kitchen busy washing plates. She said Hello as she came in and from the living room right away began talking about her day, about all the telephone calls she had had to channel. She tells him too about a letter from her brother who has been living in France for a long time.

From the living room she explains: 'He has opened a restaurant in Lyons and asks if I want to go and work with him for a while. He says I'd earn well and could soon put some money aside.'

Meantime Baratto has finished what he is doing and now is going through the living room, fanning his head with a fan in the shape of a spatula. Still fanning himself he makes his way in silence towards the spiral stair, and Marta shouts after him crossly: 'I was talking to you, did you notice?' Then she hears him shut the bedroom door; she stands there and wonders if something odd hasn't happened.

She looks round and sees that the table has been cleared, the kitchen window is half open, her food is on the cooker, like every evening. The street lamp in front of the window throws yellow light on to the ceiling. Marta thinks everything is normal.

After eating she is tired with the long day, she stretches out on the living room sofa to watch television. Every evening she has to watch television till late so as to forget the chatter of the telephone and the voices she has had in her ear for so many hours — and that is why she sleeps on the sofa in the living room while her husband sleeps at the top of the spiral stair. But this evening she has watched the television programmes listlessly, milling over what has happened, and towards eleven decides to call her friend Cristina to tell her about it.

On the phone she says: 'I was talking to him and — him — not a word — as if I didn't exist. And then he fans his head. Isn't it odd?'

Her friend Cristina answers: 'With all your admirers I told you to be careful. Maybe he's fed up and doesn't want to speak to you any more.'

Marta says: 'I don't know what to do. My brother has written to me from Lyons asking me to go and work with him. I could go there — just to get away from the factory. But how can I tell Baratto if he doesn't speak to me?'

Her friend Cristina suggests: 'Keep calm and wait for him to get over it. Or else leave him — why not? It does men good to be left by their wives.'

Marta has been asleep for some hours when Baratto gets up and crosses the living room on tiptoe. The country school where he teaches is rather far away and he has to leave home at dawn.

At dawn on his bike he crosses the deserted city to the war memorial on the bridge over the big river. He has to pass an old hotel squeezed under the arch of the bridge, and with the flat morning light the bits of mould on the hotel walls are more noticeable. Behind it are the overhead railway wires lost in the shadow. He accelerates to take a curve over a level crossing. Then on the road which runs along the river looks for something far off on the other tree-covered bank.

In the afternoon he goes for a training run on the banks of the River Trebbia which have become a 'recreational area' all covered with asphalt, and where there are always people in tracksuits running like him. Running right along the bank one reaches a group of old houses and there there is a big grey abandoned house which some call the haunted house. The left-hand corner of the big house has an odd air because behind its edge there opens up a little slope plunging down into a scrap heap which — seen from the road against the light — looks like a cosmic hole.

Passing by, Baratto has stopped to look at the corner of that house. He shuts one eye to have a better look at it. He raises one leg, scratching the calf of the other leg with his foot, and stays poised like that swaying with a meditative air and one eye closed.

Further on if you turn to the right you come to an inn which is pretty well known locally. This is a workingmen's cooperative of which this same Baratto is a member and consists of a large room used as a bar with a bowling alley behind under a pergola. About half past five the members of the cooperative begin to arrive to drink a few glasses of wine together and tell one another the news of the day — and a huge man with a little head has just arrived and is telling them: 'Well, I tell you, I was going past on my moped and I see him there on one leg and with one eye shut looking at the corner of that house. Oh I know it's a funny corner. But when I passed close to him and said Hello, well, it was like I hadn't said anything. He must still be there looking at the corner if you ask me.'

By now almost all the regulars of the inn have arrived. One of them, the gym teacher Berté tells them: 'I spoke to his headmaster and he says that even in school Baratto doesn't answer when people speak to him. It's a serious business, you know. It simply isn't legal for someone not to speak in school.'

An individual, Bicchi by name, with a stye on one eye says: 'Of course, I saw how he left the match and then he didn't want to speak to the trainer. As if he had taken leave of his senses from one minute to the other.'

The old bartender at the workingmen's cooperative interrupts to say: 'That's another story — obviously he was fed up with playing rugby. But in school Baratto teaches PE and then what need has he to talk? All he needs to do is use his whistle.'

The gym teacher Berté sighs: 'His headmaster says that if there was an inspection he could find himself in trouble for not having reported the matter to the school board. A person who doesn't talk may also be unable to understand or to want to. One never knows. That's why it is against the law not to speak — in education.'

Everybody in the inn begins to discuss the case very pleased to have such an interesting subject of conversation. Among the others there are three male nurses who along with Baratto have formed a voluntary support group for former mental-home patients. That means that sometimes they take former mental-home patients for a trip by bus to amuse them, at other times they go with them to have supper in a restaurant in the country, and in summer they take them to the swimming pool and teach them to swim in various styles. The three nurses are worried because Baratto has absented himself from the last meetings of the group called to finalise the programme for April, and wonder: 'What can have happened to him? Can he be depressed?'

Someone puts forward this thesis: 'Maybe he's got tired of always having to speak to people and answer them. It's a right bore if you think about it — always having to answer when they speak to you. But you always have to answer. Personally I admire Baratto.'

The man who has spoken is the old bartender at the workingman's cooperative who is often tired of having to speak to the customers. Many people in the inn find his observation very accurate and they now drink a glass of wine to the bartender's health.

Baratto lives in a district of houses divided into apartments, where they have only recently built enormous tower blocks, asphalt playgrounds and a big food supermarket. The front door of his house is always open because of a damaged lock, and even the door of his apartment is almost always open because since he has stopped talking it is as if Baratto is annoyed by shut doors.

The Tuesday after the first week of silence two members of the cooperative, Berté and Bicchi, decided to look in on Baratto to see if it was possible to help him to snap out of his mute state. But they found the door open and the apartment empty.

On the stairs they met an old pensioner busy watering a pot of azaleas, who began to speak to them about the weather and how the spring is a long time in coming — but about the neighbour upstairs the pensioner knew nothing.

On Wednesday, coming back from one of his training sessions on the banks of the Trebbia, Baratto met Bicchi's wife waiting for him on the stairs. In the dusty light of the stairs the blonde woman dressed in red came towards him and said: 'Bicchi told me you don't talk any more. You ought to know that I have always been very fond of men who don't talk. I find them irresistible, I confess.'

Baratto examined her, stopping to look at her neck and breast a little in the shade of the communal landing. She was saying to him: 'Listen, would you take me for a ride on your bike one of these days?' But at that moment the pensioner from the floor below came out and began to talk to the woman about the weather. Meanwhile Baratto went back into his apartment. Bicchi's wife — somewhat disappointed — went off, walking past the pensioner who was still talking to her about the weather.

Thursday was a rainy day. Baratto didn't go running. Those three male nurses from the voluntary support group for former inmates of mental homes came to look him up. Coming in they found him in the process of getting dressed with the air of having been asleep up to that moment. Without more ado they explained that he can't get out of his commitments like this. They added that refusing to talk is an easy way out when there are so many problems to be solved in the real world. Without showing that he was aware of them, Baratto withdrew into the bathroom to finish dressing. So the three continued their peroration from behind the bathroom door saying: 'If something is wrong let's speak about it, let's talk things over. But to keep silent the way you are doing isn't very rational.'

After half an hour the three nurses opened the door to find the bathroom empty and the window wide open. Baratto had got out through the bathroom window on to a terrace which gives access to the stairs, then by the stairs had left the house and gone off on his motorbike minding his own business.

For a few days no one else came to try to persuade him and meantime the weather set fine. One afternoon, finding the door open, there enters Baratto's apartment an old schoolmate of his who has heard talk of his recent muteness. This person is a lawyer who has lately become a preacher with the Jehovah's Witnesses. He has come to persuade Baratto and enters the living room with a briefcase full of pamphlets relating to his work of redemption.

Baratto has just come back from one of his training sessions on the banks of the Trebbia, completely naked and still sweaty, he looks the visitor over with staring eyes. The old schoolmate refers to their far-off friendship and to his present activity as preacher, but the naked man continues to stare at him as if he did not understand his words. Then the lawyer produces his pamphlets and, laying them out on the table, explains: 'I learned that you are shut up in yourself and don't want to speak to anyone, perhaps because of some disappointment. Certainly life is like that — there are disappointments. But we can assure you that the coming of the kingdom of God is a serious matter — clearly spelt out. That is the road to finding yourself again if you are willing to let yourself be helped. Are you prepared, Baratto, to let yourself be helped and to become a Jehovah's Witness too?'

The lawyer waits a long time for an answer. He consults his watch, poses the question again a couple of times, and finally he seems to see some reaction to his words. As if he were falling asleep, the naked man has let himself collapse on to a chair, with eyes shut and holding his breath. Then he remains seated like that with eyes shut, not breathing.

More confused than before, the lawyer decides to wind up the meeting speedily with these words: 'Very well, I think we have understood each other. Read our pamphlets and you will understand better. I'll get my secretary to phone you.'

Leaving the apartment, he stops to reflect, somewhat perplexed, in front of a pot of azaleas on the landing. And here suddenly he finds himself facing an old pensioner who is saying to him: 'I think spring has really come — at last. This morning in the flower bed down there I saw that the dandelions have come out.'

Every Saturday afternoon Baratto goes to the supermarket near his house to get the food for the week. This he continues to do during his period of muteness. However, before going to do the shopping, his habits lead him towards the centre of the city to draw money from the cash dispenser at a bank. Neither to shop in a supermarket nor to draw money from a cash dispenser is it necessary to speak, everything happens in peaceful silence.

However, wandering in peaceful silence through the streets of the city centre, it often happens that he loses himself as he wanders about looking at everything that meets his eyes. He stops to look at the people, the houses, the keystones, the sky and the gutters. Which notably slows down his walk home and sometimes when he turns back the supermarket near his house is already shut.

One Saturday afternoon, his wife has been waiting for him at home for hours, she has to talk to him. As she waited for him she watched television until the sun set. Now from the street there come the noise of passing buses, the shouts of quarrelling children, and the sky is becoming reddish. From other apartments come the sounds of other television sets turned on and the voice of an announcer reading the news of the day.

Tired of waiting, Marta telephones her friend Cristina to tell her what is happening. On the telephone she explains: 'I went to a fortune teller and the cards say that I have a most important chance that mustn't be lost. I think it's that invitation from my brother to work in his restaurant in Lyons. In the cards there was a man I haven't seen for a long time, a journey and a lot of money coming my way. It can't be anything else.'

Her friend Cristina replies: 'Then what are you waiting for? I would come to France with you too if I could.'

Marta sighs: 'Yes, I think I'll go there. But how shall I tell Baratto who pays no attention to anyone any more? I can't go away without telling him.'

Her friend Cristina suggests: 'If he doesn't listen to you write him a letter. You see everyone has their own destiny. If he wants to be mute let him be mute and you go your own way.'

Marta says: 'You're right. Next week I'll give notice to the factory then I'll buy myself a couple of nice suitcases and take the train. Obviously that's how my destiny wants it.'

About suppertime that same day a couple of old pensioners are going home. The two live under Baratto's apartment, the husband is the one who looks after the pot of azaleas on the landing. The street they are going along continues in perspective between two rows of street lamps, which are lighting up now, against the reddish sky. And when they get to the end they find Baratto standing there with his head in the air; he is looking at a lamp that has just been lit.

As they pass the pensioners greet him. Without replying to their greeting he begins to follow them with a rapt air. He follows the two to the front door of the house where he lives and follows them up the stairs, still in silence. At the door of his apartment the pensioner turns to speak to him, telling him that someone has gone and sat on his pot of azaleas and that this has upset him a lot. He asks Baratto: 'Who can it have been?'

While the pensioner is talking, his wife goes into the apartment to turn on the light. Without answering the man, Baratto follows the woman and goes into the apartment of the two pensioners. They are surprised to see him make his way in silence into their living room. They run into the living room and see him sway as he looks about him. For the moment they do not know what to do, but then they smile, happy that Baratto has come to visit them. And they politely invite him to sit down in an armchair: 'Please, make yourself comfortable.'

Baratto sits down. From that moment he stays in the house of the two pensioners for about seven months, almost always sitting in the same armchair watching television along with them or else listening to them talking. That is to say, except in the morning when he goes to school, in the afternoon when he goes to do his shopping, and in the evening when he goes up to his own apartment to clear the table which his wife continues to lay every day.

Baratto has always been a gym teacher with a high reputation, and in past years he has also given refresher courses for other teachers. Now during his teaching periods he lets his pupils play freely at basketball and meantime listens raptly to the noise of the ball on the linoleum, the thud of the footsteps, the echo of the boys' cries. Or else he stops to watch the shadows growing longer on the floor of the gym and change direction little by little in the course of the morning. Every so often he gives a whistle at random, to which however the boys pay no attention.

Between one lesson and another, like the other teachers, he too goes and sits in the so-called reception room, which is a big room with a table in the middle, bookcases and small cupboards on the walls. Here his colleagues read the paper, correct exercises or fill out the register, exchanging from time to time some gossip about the events of the day. Baratto begins to look at the headlines in a paper which is there in front of him, but very soon he falls asleep, leaning on the table with his arms folded.

In the early afternoon, when it is time for the school to shut, all the teachers have gone home and in the school there are only the janitors, who are cleaning up, the headmaster and the young secretary, who are getting ready to leave. But now a bald janitor comes running along the corridor pursuing the headmaster to tell him: 'Sir, we can't lock up because Baratto isn't to be found.' And since just at that moment another janitor comes up to confirm the news, the headmaster appears very surprised and says: 'Just explain to me what is going on.'

The janitor who has just come up explains in humble tones: 'You see, he falls asleep.' Immediately the bald janitor intervenes to clear the matter up: 'After lessons are over we have to wake him up and send him home. Usually he sleeps in the reception room, but the other day he fell asleep in the gym. Now there is his bike outside so he hasn't left, but we don't know where he has gone to sleep.'

From the mouth of the headmaster, who is more and more surprised, there come the following words in falsetto: 'Find me this individual at once.' The two janitors linger because they don't know what to do, but almost at once the voice of the school secretary is heard calling out to say: 'They're found him!'

The closet where the implements for cleaning the school are kept is long and narrow with walls covered with white tiles. On a shelf on the wall there is an old radio no longer in use, and under the shelf Baratto is sleeping in the shade on a camp bed that has somehow or other turned up there.

Two janitors are remarking that this is the best place for sleeping in the whole school where it is so boring in fact that one could feel like sleeping all the time. The headmaster and the secretary make their way through the janitors. But on the threshold the headmaster gives a start and exclaims: 'But he is naked!'

The janitors smile as if giving heavy hints, but the secretary hastens to correct: 'No, no he has shorts on.'

The headmaster thinks things over for a little and then answers: 'Never mind, I am suspending him from teaching immediately. Things like this can't be allowed. Miss, come to the office and right away I will dictate a letter to the school board suspending him.'

Laughing merrily, the janitors go to waken the peaceful sleeper, while the young secretary pursues her superior along the corridor, begging him not to suspend poor Baratto. As a means of persuasion she adds during her pursuit: 'Don't ruin him, headmaster. After all he hasn't done anything bad.'

In the office the headmaster pays no more attention to the secretary's supplications and has already begun to dictate the letter of suspension. But suddenly something comes to mind, and he stops to look at a paperknife, which is shining in the brightness of the afternoon light. Now he is talking to himself out loud: 'First of all he doesn't speak, then he loses the register and doesn't give it a thought, and now he sleeps anywhere. What sort of a person is this Baratto?'

The secretary states that Baratto is a normal person and also nice and good, only he doesn't speak, but that isn't a defect.

After a long pause for reflection the headmaster gets up and exclaims: 'Darn it, one doesn't know what to think any more.'

Without saying anything else he picks up his briefcase and goes off, the secretary stays on asking herself whether by any chance her superior has not suddenly gone mad. In the school yard the headmaster has stopped to watch magpies flying up from a tree and meantime says to himself: 'He's someone who doesn't worry — not even about people's worries about him. What do you bet that this individual has been touched by grace?'

Until a little time ago the two old tenants Baratto lives near were in the habit of watching television from morning to night. At those times when television was not transmitting interesting programmes, the couple began to tell Baratto the story of their lives. But little by little they notice that there are not many interesting programmes on television, and that, in any case, they get more pleasure out of telling the story of their lives to their guest.

They tell him it all, episode by episode, and always begin again from the beginning without ever getting tired. Baratto listens in silence, every so often he shuts his eyes and falls asleep in the armchair.

Towards evening he goes up into his apartment to see if everything is in order. Now that his wife has gone to France to work in her brother's restaurant, following the destiny told her by the cards, he no longer has to clear the table every evening. Then he cleans the little kitchen, washing out the sink where there are always ants that come in through the window, changes the deodoriser in the bathroom or else puts the clothes in the washing machine. Then he goes back downstairs to sit in his armchair and listen to the two pensioners taking turns to tell him the story of their lives.

On Saturday afternoon he continues to go to draw money from the cash dispenser at a bank and then goes to shop in the nearby supermarket. Having got back home, he puts the meat and the vegetables in the refrigerator, where he leaves them till they have gone bad and he can at last throw them away. In any case he is permanently invited to supper with the two pensioners, who are very happy to have him.

Often the old neighbour complains because someone has gone and sat on his pot of azaleas on the landing and asks the guest: 'But who can it be?' However this problem does not seem to interest Baratto, who remains silent.

After the time when he was found sleeping in the closet for cleaning things, he has regularly gone back to school every day. But one morning he finds a fair-haired janitor at the main door who makes signs to send him away. Baratto stands watching him in the middle of the courtyard, then with bent head goes back to his bike. But the other no sooner disappears than he tries to enter the school building again.

That same morning he tries to get back in several times, but is always surprised by the fair-haired janitor who comes running up making gestures to send him away. Finally a janitor friend of his intervenes to explain that the headmaster has put him on sick leave so that he can get treatment. At the main door the janitor says: 'Take it easy, Baratto. There's a supply teacher — go home and get treatment.'

So in the end he stops trying to get back into the school building. Naturally he doesn't know that all his attempts have been watched by the headmaster hidden behind a window. And he goes off on his bike, while the other (the headmaster) continues to wonder if Baratto has really had the blessing of being without worries, without the buzz of internal phrases, free from this continual raving that everybody carries about inside them.

A little later in the office, turning to the secretary, the headmaster begins to make the following reflections: 'He is like a shadow that passes without worrying that he is a shadow. An appearance which is already a disappearance. As if nothing in him was agitated about proving something.'

The secretary replies that she sincerely hasn't understood half of what the headmaster has been trying to say. The headmaster looks out of the window, wondering what all this means and what the sentences he has just uttered mean. Beyond the window one can see blackbirds flying about round the Lombardy poplars at the bottom of the school courtyard.

Meanwhile the shadow in question is on his way home through a district of new blocks of houses completely bare of people, animals, shops or bars. Passing through it one sees only bus stops and cars parked along the pavements. On the dual carriageway there is a lot of dazzling light at this time of day, but it is a colourless light. Further on a supermarket with the prices of goods on special offer on all the windows. Then boys in plastic jackets standing about in front of a bar. With his helmet on his head and sitting upright on his bike he passes by looking at them. A make-believe clock hanging at a street corner tries to tell him the time.

The season for holidays and summer tourist trips is about to begin. This year the gym teacher Berté doesn't feel like going on holiday with someone who talks too much or else talks without saying anything — as usually happens. So he turns to Baratto, asking him to go on a trip somewhere with him on their bikes.

During their meeting on the banks of the Trebbia, Baratto did not reply to the proposals of his friend who kept running behind him during his training sessions. But some days later he turns up punctually under his house, at eight o'clock, for the appointment set up by Berté. So the two set off one morning on two identical bikes, helmets on their heads and no precise goal.

On the first day of silence they go aimlessly about the countryside in a south-easterly direction and in the evening near Guastalla they see in the distance the bridge over the River Po. Before the bridge, hothouse cultivation in long nylon huts and, after the bridge, a dead straight road between two lines of poplars which block the view. When they reach the ring road of Guastalla — with cobbles, colonnades, fine houses of other centuries — two female Japanese tourists with little umbrellas are passing under the colonnades.

According to Berté it must have been these two Japanese ladies who awoke Baratto's interest in foreign tourists and in particular in Japanese ones. The fact is that next day in Mantua, early in the morning, Baratto begins to observe them a great deal in the street, sometimes stopping to contemplate groups of tourists as if he had never seen any in his life. Then he also takes to following a bus of theirs without paying any more attention to the instructions of his travelling companion. Finally he wants to join a mixed Japanese–American group visiting the old ducal palace, and Berté has to resign himself to going with him.

By coincidence the bus of the mixed Japanese–American group is parked in front of the hotel near the railway station where the two motor cyclists have found rooms. The moment he wakes up in the morning, Baratto puts on his helmet and gets on to his bike to follow that bus, pursued by Berté, who certainly did not expect a move of this kind.

With a rapt air he follows the bus along roads and motorways up to the Swiss frontier and then on to Lake Constance. Here he forces Berté to go in search of a room in a tiny pension in a little street on the outskirts, where the two will have to sleep in the same bed, but not far from the hotel where the mixed group is staying. And along with Berté, after supper, he goes for a walk through the gardens by the side of the lake, always keeping an eye in the dusk on the Japanese tourists from the bus, who are also walking in those little alleys decked with giant flowers.

The next day, still absentminded and silent, he follows them to the city of Freiburg im Breisgau. He gets Berté to book rooms in the old hotel in which the mixed group from the bus are guests. He follows a group of Japanese on an evening visit to the Italian icecream parlours scattered at the nerve centres of the old town. He buys an icecream and, like them, feels like eating while walking on the cobbles of the old square in front of the cathedral, where some old Japanese gentlemen begin to recognise him and to bow to him. At the end of the evening Baratto, too, is bowing to the old Japanese gentlemen.

Next morning he follows their bus on a rapid tour of the Black Forest above the town. He returns with them and in the evening follows them to a Gasthaus where he attentively watches them eating sausages. At this point Berté, Baratto's inseparable companion, has also learnt to bow to Japanese gentlemen.

And the day after, too, across rolling landscapes strewn with little lakes, Baratto and Berté follow on behind their friends' bus to the city of Heidelberg. They arrive at a parking place at the foot of the hill on which the famous castle rises. They get off their bikes and here Baratto gives signs that he feels very good — not only by the large gestures of deep breathing he begins to make, but by the expression of his eyes with which he scans the tourists. You would think he has finally found his own people, and feels himself like those foreigners who are led about in flocks, looked after by guides who recite strange litanies of names, lost in the great tourist mystery of the world.

The two travellers now walk up the long climb topped by the castle. Now they enter the castle courtyard where a billboard receives them with these words in English: HAVE YOUR PICTURE TAKEN ON THE PICTURESQUE GROUND OF THE FAMOUS HEIDELBERG CASTLE.

The castle with its towers and old walls and drawbridges does not seem to interest Baratto. In the middle of the courtyard and next to the billboard near which a photographer with a tripod is stationed, he waits patiently for the Japanese tourists to come and have a group photograph taken. And when they arrive, he manages, with many respectful bows, to have himself photographed in their company.

The old Japanese gentlemen received him courteously among them and by signs proposed to him to pose beside a tiny widow, who reaches up almost to his stomach. This evidently because the widow is the only unaccompanied person in the group, which is made up of married couples. And Baratto accepted the proposal with such joyful expressions on his face that afterwards the tiny widow never stopped showing him her gratitude. So much so that she drew him away from the group and now — with numerous bows and signs with her head — invites him to the restaurant in front of the castle.

The old Japanese gentlemen smile to Baratto and make signs of goodwill to induce him to accept the invitation. After some hesitation, in the end he accepts, and now he is leaving the castle and crossing a lawn under old oaks among many other bewildered tourists and following the tiny widow.

Berté watches the two from a distance and sees them enter the restaurant in friendly conversation made up of gestures and bows. The two pass a good part of the afternoon seated opposite each other, drinking Coca-Cola and eating slices of cake. Through the window of the restaurant Berté sees that the Japanese widow is talking without stopping and very very fast in her own language, probably telling Baratto the whole story of her life. And Baratto from time to time opens his eyes wide, at other times he shakes his head, or else stretches out a hand and gives her a pat on the arm.

To Berté's eyes the widow seems flattered by these pats. Each time indeed she fends them off, shrugging with a smile, then she begins once more to talk very very fast in her own language. Perhaps she is a woman who has had many troubles in her life and is taking the opportunity to tell them to someone.

That Baratto understands so well ought not to surprise one. In fact he is now recovering and is beginning to think only the thoughts of others.

*

During the months of silence don't think that Baratto stopped thinking. This happens to him at times, for example when he holds his breath, but in general he has only stopped having thoughts that are a burden in his head. And if he meets someone he knows he must shake their hand or shake his head or smile when the other is talking. But such things do not demand thoughts that are actually his own thoughts, and he gets away with thinking the thoughts of others.

Then when he meets people, he limits himself to smiling when the other person shows that there's something to smile at, he frowns if there is need for it, and sometimes shows surprise to please the other person. Or else he looks elsewhere if the person talking to him is thinking thoughts too remote from him.

At the beginning of autumn, he is still a guest in the house of the two old pensioners. One evening he went up to his apartment to wash out the basin — it is full of ants which come in at the window — and now as he comes down the stairs he stops on the landing and sways. His glance shifts to search for the pensioner's pot of azaleas; when he has found it he goes and sits on it and stays sitting there with his eyes shut, without thoughts and without even the thought of being there.

In the meantime a doctor who lives opposite on the landing comes home and sees him sitting on the pot. He invites him to sit in his apartment saying that he will be more comfortable. Baratto follows him into the apartment without saying anything, one reason being that it is the doctor who talks all the time. He explains to him that he suffers from loneliness, so he is very pleased every time someone comes to visit him.

He invites Baratto to sit down in an armchair in the parlour and at once begins to tell him the story of his life.

The doctor says: 'Getting on for half-past five or six is the worst time of the day. If I come home, then it seems to me that there is a grey patina on the furniture which makes everything miserable. I put on all the lights, I've also bought this halogen lamp, but however much light you have that grey patina always remains on the furniture and the armchairs. Sometimes I have the impression that it is the dust of things that has been arriving here for all eternity, but my maid says she cleans every day.'

The living room is very big, with indirect lighting and divans in soft leather. The doctor is a middle-aged man, a little bald and with grey hair ruffled at the temples. He says that, in that town, the more people you know, the more you feel an outsider, and since he knows almost all of them he feels like an Eskimo. Moreover he has been left by a girl who one day said to him: 'Living with you is like being dead.'

As he tells this story the doctor smiles. Baratto, seeing him smile, smiles too, and shakes his head merrily. Then the doctor offers him a big cigar, and the two sit there smoking cigars and drinking white wine until suddenly the telephone rings in another room.

When the doctor comes back, his grey hair is all dishevelled and standing up like wings on his temples. He explains that on the telephone there was that girl who left him, and he didn't want to talk to her but she wanted to talk to him and explained why she wanted to talk to him and so they were on the telephone for three hours. Basically the girl had wanted to say this to him: that he had just made her waste time in the best years of her life.

Halfway through this story Baratto falls asleep in the armchair. He wakes up suddenly in the night and the doctor appears in front of him in dressing gown and bedroom slippers, with very thin legs and his hair standing on end on his temples. He asks Baratto: 'Can I put on a light?'

Baratto pays no attention to him and he puts on all the lights in the parlour. He stays there looking at the effect produced by the halogen lamps, saying to himself: 'It's better with a little light — really better.'

Now Baratto has begun to smoke another cigar and the doctor sits down beside him and begins to reflect: 'I know that I look like a failure. But there's nothing to be surprised at because my parents before me looked like failures — both my father and my mother. I have a big son and he also looks like a failure — he has a face like an eel in a fridge.'

The doctor continues: 'But what I say is — is it maybe all make-believe? For instance this city a piece of make-believe, the women who make us suffer a piece of make-believe, work a piece of make-believe, our looking like failures another piece of make-believe? Is it maybe all an epic production, a dream from which we don't manage to wake up? But I'll tell you something else — is the light not also maybe a piece of make-believe? And the sounds we hear, the things we touch, the dark and the night, could it not perhaps all be an immense piece of make-believe? A whole comedy of appearances that makes us believe all sorts of things and instead none of it is true?'

At that precise moment both of them notice that it is dawn already, and then they go out on to the terrace of the house to see the sun rise. In a house opposite a window lights up behind lowered blinds; both of them hope that there is a naked woman to spy on through the blinds.

The sky is getting lighter, in the distance someone is raising a shutter. Both of them think that out there everything is functioning — there are even swallows flying round the trees facing them, as if something were about to happen.

Then bells in the distance. Who rings the bells? Who raises the shutter?

Not far away there is a district with new tower blocks where silence reigns. The phone box at the corner. Someone starts up a motorbike and drives off. Both of them think that the comedy of appearances always goes on out there and never stops.

At this point however the doctor notices that he is thinking Baratto's thoughts, even if in fact Baratto has no real thoughts of his own. Rather they are the thoughts of others that come into his mind — those of someone passing in the street, of someone raising a shutter, of someone starting up a motorbike in the distance.

Thanks to so many people thinking the same things, the phrase 'It is dawn' really means that it is dawn with all its different appearances. And thanks to Baratto who, as he gets better, begins to have only the thoughts of others, this piece of make-believe of the dawn now appears to be true to the doctor as well.

One afternoon on a Saturday that was already wintry, he went out as usual to go shopping in the nearby supermarket. After doing his shopping he waits with his trolley to pay at the checkout and comes out with two baskets of purchases. At the door of the supermarket he meets a blonde woman who says to him: 'Look who's here! Long time no see! I told you what I felt — why didn't you come and see me?'

He examined her and then made his way in silence homewards, followed by the woman who continues to talk. They are going up the stairs in the house where Baratto lives and where the woman follows him right into his apartment. Here she watches him putting the food he has bought neatly into the fridge and meanwhile says to him: 'Don't you like me? If you don't like me there's no need to put on such an act. But to keep me dangling for six months without a word — does that seem right?'

Baratto shakes his head and smiles, he has found a grub in the greens.

The door to the apartment has remained open because, since he has been mute, it's as if Baratto finds shut doors tiresome. So now two men come freely into the apartment and stop to look around them in the living room.

One of them is a weightlifter who enters the world championships; lately he has begun to be afraid of death and goes around telling everyone, and today he wanted to come and tell Baratto. The other person is a little thin man with a pock-marked face, a professor of German, who follows the weightlifter everywhere and advises him; he is called Professor Crone and he is also a medium.

The two want to know why Baratto no longer comes to their bar to play cards on Thursdays and the blonde woman comments: 'Oh, he's someone who hides himself away.'

The weightlifter says: 'I envy him. Without children, a good salary, without worries. I have to watch out for everything because at any moment something can happen. If I cross the street I can pull a muscle and fuck up the championships for myself. I can't even go with women — if I come across one with an illness I fuck up the championships for myself. Every second something can happen — did you ever think of that? Eh? What does the professor say?'

Professor Crone nods.

Baratto has finished putting away his shopping and sprinkling the edges of the basin in the little kitchen. Without paying any attention to the others, he goes off down the stairs and the others follow him chatting away. When he rings at the door of the two pensioners the doctor's door opens instead and the doctor appears and calls to them: 'We're here — come in.'

Through Baratto the doctor and the two old pensioners have become friends and often pass the evenings together, telling one another the story of their lives in turn. The two pensioners also give the doctor a lot of advice concerning the pain of solitude.

In the doctor's apartment, seated on the soft leather divans, they all begin to drink white wine and to smoke cigars which the host distributes. The blonde woman smokes too and doesn't stop laughing because of all that smoke coming out of her mouth. Alongside her Professor Crone drinks with a faraway look, slowly pulling hairs out of his ears.

After a cold supper prepared by the doctor, they light up cigars again and start listening to records while discussing their various musical preferences. The doctor likes jazz while the blonde woman doesn't understand it and the two pensioners prefer classical music provided it is played well. The weightlifter says he has no time to listen to music, because of all the things that can happen at any moment. And Professor Crone says nothing, he is busy poking in his mouth for bits of food.

Someone suggests watching television but the pensioners and the doctor are against it. Then they all decide to tell the story of their lives, and the blonde women begins saying: 'I'm fed up with going to the match every Sunday only because Bicchi wants me to see him play. Specially since he has fallen in love with another woman and is crazy about her.'

So she tells the story of her husband, Bicchi by name, in love with a woman whom he always sees at a service station on the motorway. When he comes past in the pickup that woman is always there smoking in the bar, looking out of the window at the reflections of the neon lights on the courtyard. And since she smokes Marlboro cigarettes and Bicchi doesn't know her name, he calls her 'the woman who smokes Marlboros' and does nothing but talk about the woman who smokes Marlboros. One evening a colleague of his said: 'I'd give that one a good cigarette to smoke,' and Bicchi tried to throttle him. Afterwards they dissolved the contract cleaning firm they had together, and now Bicchi is without work — all because of the woman who smokes Marlboros.

It is the doctor's turn to speak and he says: 'I was married for a long time to a woman I didn't understand. I didn't understand what she expected day after day, why she bought so many clothes, why she did her hair and made up so carefully. Often I looked at her secretly to see if she still had the same face, the same eyes, the same colour of hair. I always expected her to come home one day and be someone completely different and not recognise me any more. At other times, when I looked at her, I saw birds in my wife's face — her eyebrows were two swallows, her nose a little sparrow, her mouth a hawk gliding with soft, firm wings.'

The doctor's story left them all a little puzzled — but now it is the turn of the weightlifter to speak and he says: 'Don't you think about death? I think about it all the time and can't sleep for it. I think that when we are dead we stay dead for a very long time, for such an infinite time that it makes my head spin, I get fits of giddiness. And it ends up with me losing my form, do you understand? Because even lost sleep can weaken me, even a cold, and then the championships go up in smoke. Ah, we are fragile, very fragile.'

Then he tells them that along with Professor Crone he holds spiritualist sessions to ask the dead what may happen and thus avoid trouble. The professor is a very great medium able to make even the most distant dead speak. 'The dead almost always speak to him,' the weightlifter adds, 'and we record them with a hi-fi stereo system which I bought for the purpose. Isn't that right, professor?'

Professor Crone nods.

At this point someone proposes holding a spiritualist session to hear the dead speak. Everyone applauds the idea and the lights are lowered and the medium sits alone at a table in the shade. There is a great silence for many minutes. The professor begins to ask questions into the void facing the wall as if he were talking on the telephone: 'I can't hear very well'.

In fact no one hears anything. But then everyone begins to have the impression that there is a voice in the room, like the weak soft voice of a dead person who has not spoken for centuries. It comes from the opening of the fireplace behind a sofa.

Having fallen asleep next to the fireplace Baratto is speaking in his sleep and replying to the professor's questions. They all become aware of this and are excited, they encourage the professor to go on asking questions. And Crone asks: 'Tell me what you are thinking about.'

The sleeper begins with confused phrases and says he can't reply because his thoughts aren't there but elsewhere. When the professor asks where they are, he replies that time goes by and thoughts go by and who knows where thoughts go.

After a lot of phrases like this, the professor asks him to explain himself a little better, they want to know what he has in his head. Then Baratto, sitting up like a sleepwalker, touches himself on the temple and replies that there is nothing in there, in his head. Everything is going on out there.

Someone in the audience wants to know: 'Out where?' And sitting motionless but half opening his eyes he answers: 'Out in the air where the phrases that come to mind go about and so a person can say something.'

Then it is the doctor who intervenes to ask: 'Baratto, you have been mute for so many months, but what did you have in your head all that time?'

The blonde woman comments excitedly: 'Ah, it's so interesting to know what goes on in other people's heads.'

Still with his eyes shut and motionless Baratto replies to the question with these words: 'Phrases come and go and make the thoughts come which then go. Talk and talk, think and think and then there's nothing left. The head is nothing — it all happens in the open.'

At this point the weightlifter makes a comment with a critical air: 'Hey, are we sure he isn't having us on? As far as I'm concerned I've had enough of listening to this crap.'

The old pensioner protests: 'Shut up, you, and don't talk nonsense! You seem immature to me, if you really want to know.'

The weightlifter replies with a sneer: 'Oh so I'm immature? Dear grandpa, you don't know me. For your information, I have taken part in two world championships and have also read books of philosophy. Isn't that so, Professor Crone?'

Professor Crone nods, but suddenly the blonde woman speaks up: 'Give over and shut up everyone! Look he's waking up.'

Behind the divan Baratto gives a big yawn with deep throaty noises. Getting up he touches his knee and murmurs to himself: 'Oh my meniscus is hurting again!' He yawns again and stretches, then he wakes up completely. Now he gives a big smile and asks if he has spoken well.

They all applaud. And this is how Baratto began to speak again.

*CONDITIONS OF LIGHT
ON THE VIA EMILIA*

Luciano Capelli and I often met the signwriter Emanuele Menini and often listened to his thoughts about the state of things along the road he lived on, the via Emilia.

Emanuele Menini lived for twenty years on this road and being a landscape painter he knew very well how the light falls from the sky, how it touches and envelops things.

The road on which Menini lives passes through several cities of medium size and running through one of the least ventilated plains in the world reaches the sea. It's a dividing line between the high ground and the low ground traced I don't know how long ago, which never offers very distant horizons because it is shut off on one side by the profile of the hills and, on the other, by fields which rise up almost to the level of the eyes.

The profile of the hills rises up in eroded gullies and crests towards mountains depopulated in some parts, often bare, with woods where desolate hunters occasionally wander in search of vanished game. It is this line of mountains that blocks all the winds from the east, the rising currents of air that come from the sea, thus making these parts so little ventilated.

On certain clear days, by climbing the mountain and looking towards the long road, one can see a layer — bluish or pearly depending on the seasons — suspended almost permanently over the plain. That is the cloud in which people live in these parts, a cloud in which every kind of luminosity is dispersed in myriads of rays.

There are unbroken lines of traffic on most of the long road for many hours each day — and for a large part of its route it travels between two pieces of scenery formed by billboards, long factory sheds, service stations, emporiums selling furniture and lamps, car showrooms, car dumps, bars, restaurants, little houses in bright colours, or else districts with high blocks that have risen in the midst of the countryside.

Roundabout the air is almost always bright with changing tones, caused by the fine dust, by the traces of the fumes from the motors, by the layers of powdered material from the asphalt surface and from the wheeltracks, as well as by the vapours given off by the soil of chalky and clayey marl. So the light striking down from above is engulfed in a layer of atmosphere much denser and heavier than the others; and that cancels or greatly reduces the differences with the daytime shadows, because of the great dispersion of the luminous rays which are continually diverted or casually reflected, and which envelop everything in a cloud of glare and rays.

Naturally there are many differences between the ways in which the light is dispersed at the different times of day and in the different seasons. Since these parts are an extremely ancient gulf of marshes, filled for the most part with clay, where the rains run off or evaporate without being retained by the soil, they are also a zone with some of the thickest seasonal mists.

So, because of the thick mists which rise from the ground, the cloud of reflected light on the long road often seems opaque or ash-grey in humid seasons. However it is almost always iridescent in the hottest months and in summer, for instance, in the morning a field of cabbages can present itself to the eyes in a fluorescent green, a service station and a factory shed can appear as tremulous as a mirage, while the clear sky is all pearl-coloured up to the zenith.

Only when the sun is low on the horizon does it become possible to make out clearly the shadows on the ground, the contours of things, and to look at things without having the view of them obfuscated by glare in the air. And at night on the long road not many stars are to be seen, one even forgets that in other parts of the planet skies thickly populated with lights are a normal sight. Here, up high, on summer nights the lights of the Milky Way and the Plough and the Pleiades are almost always lost, impossible to find, their scintillations muffled by the fog on these parts where there are so few winds.

The signwriter Emanuele Menini had often reflected on all this even if he had confined himself to observing a short stretch of that road between his house and the bar five hundred metres from his house, there and back.

Just outside the house where Menini lives you find yourself in front of a bridge over which a railway line passes. On the other side of the bridge the long road goes on between two lines of low houses and further on the space widens out towards districts made up of tall buildings all sharp against the sky.

To Menini that ring road, always crowded in the morning with motors and people going out to shop, often appeared — when seen against the light and from the other side of the bridge — merely a fog full of beams of light. And in his thoughts he saw that the lines of cars on the tar, together with the inhabitants in the streets, the bushes that had grown in a crack in the pavement, the leaves of a big plane tree next to a service station, all joined in a vast movement of convection and fluctuation of the stagnant air, through which there passed waves and whirlpools of traffic.

What he saw at that moment was a blend of air in which there moved shadows drowned in the dispersed light. Menini said: 'Light that has shattered.'

Going on beyond the bridge every morning he crossed the point where the cloud is thicker, because the road is narrower between these low houses with little shops. Here the buses which often occupied all the tarred surface, the people waiting for the bus, the people going shopping or into the bar, all were caught up in the ebb and flow with more intense whirlpools and eddies. And in the ebb and flow compressed into a narrow space, the signwriter began to detect a tremor in the air which made everything unstable, swaying around him as he himself swayed with the others.

This was the everyday tremor which comes as morning begins, something that transports you and which you can't resist, which Menini compared to a state of intoxication.

Then at the point where the road widens out and is crossed by a four-lane ring road, he often noticed that a percussive wave passes through the air as if through a combustion chamber. In fact in the larger space the tremor of the ebb and flow which was compressed at the previous point bursts out, the traffic suddenly accelerates, the vehicles go off at full speed towards the traffic lights. And when you hear those trucks with trailers accelerating, bringing to its peak the tremor which makes everything sway, you see very clearly that here it is difficult to escape from the intoxication.

According to Menini, what happened at that point was like when drunks become violent. The same went for those drunks going past in their vehicles.

Further on, at the bar where Menini went every day, the view opens out towards the perspective of a long four-lane main road. And standing at the door of his bar at various times of the year, the signwriter saw there, at the other end, a white mist on a knoll where an imposing cedar of Lebanon dominates the traffic. The silhouette of the great tree was always black, while the lines of vehicles down there were a mass of imprecise shapes with luminous contours lost in that milky fog.

Once Menini had walked as far as that knoll because the great cedar of Lebanon had made him think of God, and there an idea had come into his head.

The first time that Luciano Capelli took me to meet Menini one Sunday in January, in his usual bar, he looked me over for a long time and said at last: 'So you are someone who writes. Well done! I shall be content if you write what I say — that way my breath won't be so wasted.'

And he immediately began to tell the story of that walk to the knoll taken because the great cedar of Lebanon made God come into his mind.

When he had arrived there, turning round, he had noticed that he could no longer see the cloud that enwraps the traffic down his way, because it was no longer against the light. He had gone on beyond the knoll and had seen that even when he looked ahead he could not see the cloud on the road, because beyond the knoll there are no more obstacles and nothing screens the rays of the sun in the open countryside.

Turning back he had passed in front of a modern cemetery where they were taking the coffin of some dead person from these suburbs. He had stopped between the cars to cross himself and, just at that moment, a thought had come to him.

He had thought that to see the cloud one had to be at special points — for instance on this side of that bridge. But even at those special points there was a choice of two things: either you follow the tremor or you look at it. And in these outskirts of the town to look at and see something was almost impossible.

'Why?' he asked himself. And he explained to us why: because you look and think you have seen something, but the tremor in the air immediately carries off the thought of what you have seen. So there is only the thought of rushing on in the exploded light, and you have to rush on and that is all there is to it in the everyday bustle.

He thought this was the reason why people in his district did not seem to worry at all about the cloud in which they live, a cloud you enter without noticing it and, when you are in it, it is very difficult to observe and recognise as something unusual. That Sunday in the bar, among men playing at cards and others commenting on the sports news, he summed up his conclusions thus: 'Inside this cloud we are all bound to one another by breathing. No one can breathe differently from the others and have other thoughts. And so we are all like drunks who don't know what they are doing but hold one another by the hand. I am telling you — I'm a nobody but I have lived here for twenty years.'

We were scarcely out of the bar than the signwriter pointed out to us on the side of the road a dog mangled by the traffic and said: 'Look, that is what life is like here. So when you feel the tremor in the air you must watch out. Here we live like drunks and you never know what can happen to you. So mind you don't cross the road too often. Because hereabouts everybody respects only the vehicles and thinks only of machines. And is of the opinion that if something isn't a machine it is one of the lowest forms of life.'

Another Sunday I and Luciano Capelli went by car with Menini to visit a young industrialist — a manufacturer of spiral staircases who was a relation and admirer of his. It had snowed all night and as we went towards the plain where a tile-making town stands, about thirty kilometres from the axis of the long road, everything was white and blurred by the glow of the little clouds which filled the distance.

We stopped to look at a river. The noise of the water running through the snow, the barking of the dogs in the distance, the noise of the cars passing on a nearby road, reached us muffled in space. The signwriter made this comment: 'Snow resists the tremor while rain confuses it. Because with snow there comes a little immobility in things while the rain instead hammers and drums away, and nobody can stand it any longer and everyone wants only to get off home.'

A lot of cars with skiers were passing with skis on the roofs, coming out of a curve at full speed and then losing themselves in the fog on their way to that line of mountains which runs along the long road. The skiers in the cars seemed happy and Menini said: 'They are happy off skiing because the snow makes everything a little more normal. With the white the contrasts come out more sharply and then things seem clear and tranquil.'

The great plain of the tile-making town begins not far from the point where we had stopped. There, for kilometres and kilometres, they have sliced into the hills to get clay and make it into tiles. That morning as we passed we could see slices of hill still standing on the flat white ground, spurs that rose up from the earth flattened by the bulldozers. In other places we saw nothing because the hills had all been removed, and in other places still, instead of hills, we saw immense holes dug out to get clay — big rectangular valleys surrounded by moorlands of yellowed grass.

Menini told us that when he was a child he used to go gleaning in these parts with his grandmother. They gathered heads and grains of wheat left on the ground after reaping and with them managed to make a few days' bread. Every so often during these gleaning expeditions his grandmother stopped and pissed standing up with her legs apart, scarcely lifting her wide skirt which reached to the ground. But at other times he and his grandmother went to dig clay with a spade, then with a mould they made bricks to sell to the dealers but then they stopped because the dealers only wanted industrial bricks with perfect corners.

While we were crossing a deserted spot between rows of factory sheds with courtyards in front of them all piled with tiles wrapped in nylon, Menini asked us to stop the car. In the middle of the road he pointed a finger and cried to us: 'That's where my school was,' but we only saw high buildings with windows full of US style signs which were the offices of firms making tiles in the open country. On the other side of the road a scrap heap was covered with snow and surrounded by a wire fence, further on a board warned: SHIFTING SAND.

Before arriving at the villa of the industrialist who made spiral staircases, as we passed along a little country road we saw a huge warehouse completely empty inside, all in glass, but lit up on the outside by two clusters of powerful lamps which were switched on in broad daylight. In front there was a small house in a box-like style with two Arizona cypresses on either side of the entrance.

We had stopped and Menini was looking alternately at the enormous empty and illuminated warehouse and at the two little cypresses opposite. Finally he made this announcement to us: 'These trees there are lost and dispersed because their place is on some mountain. They plant them here because they grow quickly and don't need attention. But they are lost and dispersed like me, Emanuele Manini, and almost everybody I see near where I live. You who are a writer write this in your notebook.'

That winter Sunday we arrived very late at the villa not far from the tile-making town where we were received by a woman who lived with the manufacturer of spiral staircases. The villa (since transformed) was then in the Californian style — at least such were the intentions of its owner who had had it built by a local architect.

The woman who received us was the wife of a tile millionaire, who had run away from home and come to live here in this big villa with its sloping roof and external beams of white pine, which the manufacturer of spiral staircases, according to Menini, had had built for her. He had had it built to show her his love and to convince her to leave her husband.

The young industrialist told us that day that in the vicinity there lived only millionaires — there was a millionaire every forty thousand square feet. Of himself he said: 'I made my money with spiral staircases sold all over the world — even to the Japanese. If you have an idea, making money isn't that difficult. Look at me, my father was a blacksmith and we put up the factory together. Now I'm afraid of no one, not even of the tile millionaires.'

According to Menini he was planning a trip to the United States to see if the villas in California were really made like his.

*

Emanuele Menini, in so far as he was a landscape painter, was interested above all in understanding what things that stand still look like when they are touched by light. So every day as he went to his bar in the morning and then to the warehouse where he worked, not far from the bar, he observed how things looked on the long road where he lived.

In particular in the hot months, he noticed that not only persons and cars but also things all around — though by nature still — rarely seemed immobile.

Things appeared clear-cut and peaceful only when the wind managed to break in from time to time, sweeping the air clean. But more often they were unstable and indistinct, because of a veil of little rays of light which blurred their contours and prevented him from seeing their immobility. For example he kept an eye on an old stone post on the other side of the street in front of his bar, and he always saw it with wavering contours.

In this connection the industrialist who made spiral staircases said to Menini: 'Menini, are you sure that it isn't your eyes which see things blurred? For my part I go to the factory every morning and never see any of the things you say. Won't it be better to go and see an oculist?'

Since others had already given him this advice the signwriter one day went to hospital to have his eyes examined. But it seems the oculist told him that he had better long sight than others because he didn't see clearly close up. When Menini explained to him that things always appeared with blurred contours because of the shining light, it seems the doctor replied: 'Well, maybe it's as you say. There is so much rubbish in the air. But if you pay no attention to it you don't notice it.'

This comforted the signwriter who therefore once again started his observation of things along the road.

One day he explained to me: 'I'll tell you why Menini isn't a great painter. Because if he doesn't see immobility he certainly can't manage to paint it. But there is another fact you must write down. If Menini or anyone else can't see it things are in a sorry state.'

Since he knew that Luciano was a photographer, one Sunday in March he asked him to accompany him on an exploration of the district with big houses in front of his bar, to photograph the immobile state of things (if they managed to see it). Because this is what Menini was always seeking around himself and within himself, in his thoughts, and hoped photography might help him.

He had never gone into that district. There, as he walked between extremely high white houses, he suddenly had the impression of being in a deserted gorge under the sun. The air gleamed against the white walls, the beams of light on the tar bothered his eyes, and those streets full of cars parked along the pavements — but empty of men or beasts — confused him.

He stopped to listen to the Sunday silence and felt a distant tremor which came right up to the shutters of these long blocks of houses and up to the blades of grass in a little lawn. He pointed out to Luciano the blades of grass which were oscillating slightly and then said: 'Dear Luciano, here too things are in a sorry state.'

At one end of the district there is a public garden with cement benches, a few dwarf firs and some magnolia trees. The two explorers sat down to watch the blackbirds flying about in the fine dust, some boys riding past on bikes, a gentleman taking a dog for a walk in the iridescent air.

Beyond the garden they found a little old church repainted with industrial paint, cream and purple. The signwriter wanted to go in and pray while Luciano stayed outside taking photographs.

They were going back to the usual bar and Menini set out his thoughts like this: 'Dear Luciano, I think we have to ask ourselves what is light and what is shadow so as not to leave things alone in their sorry state. I am coming to the point: you'll see lots of people going about who become furious if they happen to see something that doesn't move. For them it is normal for the light to be splintered, since it goes with the tremor and then everything moves and one must always be busy. Well, what can we say about those people who find no peace in the immobility of things. Remember, they are the majority. Ah what can we say?'

This is a question that Menini kept asking himself for a while. And once he asked us to go with him by car to take a trip in the countryside in order to find an answer.

Having left the long road and gone further into the countryside, we passed very many empty peasant houses whose inhabitants have gone to live in the little villas in acrylic colours scattered around. We found ourselves in places that were not places only rows of little villas in acrylic colours surrounded by little walls of plastic clay, which in the middle of spring threw on to the tar strange summer shadows.

In front of the little villas there were always little Arizona cypresses to decorate the entrance and often little lamps in the gardens. According to Menini these lamps too were lost and dispersed because according to him everything out of place was a poor lost thing.

The over-bright colours of the flowers in front of the doors and those acrylic paints gleaming on the walls, in contrast with the dark hues of the doors and windows, made these country places modern in some prescribed way. Any twilight uncertainty having been abolished, the colours were all sharp like in a commercial traveller's book of samples. And it seemed to us that all appearances had become objects of barter with a precise model, including the shadows and the light, the silence and the noises: they no longer depended on the time of day, on chance or fate, but solely on the model for sale.

Then we stopped in the square of a little village surrounded by polled trees and crowded by boys with mopeds parked in front of an icecream parlour. The signwriter pointed out to us things shrouded in the dispersed light of the early afternoon and showed us how everything shrouded in that light — a wall, an area of the pavement, a corner of the street invaded by beams — reminded one of buying and selling like the neon lights of advertisements.

Then he pointed out to us how these boys with their mopeds tended to gather only where there is a dispersed light full of rays which invades everything and cancels out the shadows perhaps because they are attracted by shops and by advertisements.

On the way back he wanted to stop in a little country road to reflect. This is the reflection he made: if something appears with fairly stable shadows so that the light can make the shadow breathe through the colours, instead of suffocating it in the sharp shadowless colours, that object appears to be in a sorry state. Why? He did not know why.

But he pointed to a little ditch by the side of the road. And there there were fairly motionless shadows which suddenly appeared touching to Luciano.

In the car Menini said to us: 'Where do these thoughts come from? Who knows! But it comes into my head that the explosion of neon light is like a dog barking to make us run, and we run. The same with the other splintered light which looks like neon light. That is why an unmoving, calm shadow seems unfortunate to Menini. For the feeling of immobility it puts into one when really one should run.'

Finally, as we went down the long road, he pointed out to us how the beautiful spring shadows in the ditches all had the air of waiting uselessly, too motionless for this world.

For many months I did not see the signwriter again because I went abroad. Menini felt my absence in that there was no one to write down his thoughts and he felt he was wasting his breath. All the more since Luciano was now working for a company that did lagging with asbestos fibre in the industrial warehouses, and had to get up at five every morning and be out all day; then on Sunday he had to look after his little girl and so never had time to go and meet Menini in the usual bar.

At the end of the summer the signwriter telephoned him

one night to ask him to jot down the thoughts that had come to him until such time as the gentleman writer came back. On the phone he said: 'Listen to me carefully, Luciano. Light and shade don't go well together these days because of the dirty air which doesn't give good shadows and then it gets into our lungs as well. And like drunks we try to make up for this by putting clear and lively colours everywhere, so that they can be seen better. But we get more and more drunk because the lively colours make you forget the shadows and the twilights and make you stupid — that's the fact of the matter.'

Towards the end of summer he tried to examine these views more thoroughly by observing a stretch of road near his house where the ebb and flow of the air produces a percussive wave like a combustion chamber. At that point the traffic accelerates and the cars go off at full speed to reach the lights before they turn red. And it was there, according to Menini, that the motorists, already drunk because of the tremor, became recklessly drunk.

But since they often did not manage to slow down in time when the lights went red and the other drunks impelled by the tremor started off too soon, there were very often accidents at the intersection.

In the case of an accident the signwriter observed the following: what the smashed cars at the crossroads looked like, in the light which was engulfed in layers of air thick with the effects of all the combustion, and what the people looked like who had got out of the cars to argue, they too standing there in the full exploded light and gesticulating like mad men, while other motorists held up at the intersection became furious too because of their immobility, which they found unbearable, and began to sound their horns in immensely long lines of cars, urged on by the spasmodic tremor that spreads through the suburbs at rush hour.

By observing these aspects he came to some conclusions. When there was an accident men and machines seemed to him to be stuck out there in the light and wrapped in reflections, in a great solitude on the asphalt.

And in his thoughts he saw that nothing renders bodies

isolated in space more than does the light, showing them to be definitely isolated in the same way as a kerbstone or a vase of flowers.

One day he said to Luciano: 'In the light bodies feel their isolation and would like to run off like hares. But run off where? I am coming to the point: try to look at the horizon and then tell me if someone feeling the tremor can think of the horizon and have the wish to live in its company. Impossible! You want isolation and more and more isolation even if you are already fairly isolated. And you want to run away and shut yourself up somewhere. It is the shattered light that plays this trick because it makes you run. And you want only the things that are there, slender and lively to your eyes, and there is no question of thinking about the horizon. But everything that is there — if it stays still — you at once see what it is. What is it?'

Luciano did not know and Menini told him: 'A mere nothing in the light, a mere nothing which comes in the light. That is why no one can bear immobility, they want to be rushing along all the time, and they all get furious when something holds them up. They always want to rush along as I have already told you. Write down what I have told you and then we'll talk about it.'

At the beginning of autumn it rained a lot. Almost all the flowers on Luciano's balcony were burnt because of the acidity of the rain and because of the dirty air the balcony was covered by a layer of light-brown soft mud.

Watching the crossroads Menini saw more accidents than usual, more dogs and cats pulped by the traffic, more people coming out of their houses with little masks over their mouths, more women coming out of the hairdressers with a nylon bag on their heads to protect themselves from that deadly cloud. And his lungs began to hurt more than usual, a couple of times he woke up in the morning with his mouth full of blood and he was taken to hospital.

Then the east winds came to sweep the air clean for a couple of days and it felt like being in another world.

*

Emanuele Manini was not exactly a signwriter although this was the shorthand way in which he always introduced himself. His speciality was painting panels for merry-go-rounds, pianolas and also stages in theatres when they came his way. But he had learned to paint everything and in recent years he and three other partners had hired a warehouse near the via Emilia, because their firm was commissioned to make big puppets in cardboard and comic machines with characters from strip cartoons for carnivals and American amusement parks.

It seems the Americans considered them to be craftsmen in a class of their own when it came to the creation of animated puppets. They had already consulted them over the construction of American amusement parks throughout Europe; a colossal job which would have transformed the four old craftsmen into magnates of cardboard puppets.

But Menini's real speciality always remained something else. They were landscapes, baskets of flowers, children's faces and the garlands that decorate the ring of panels at the top of merry-go-rounds, or the panels hanging at the height of the wooden horses. Above all landscapes were his passion when they had mountains covered with snow in the background, brooks meandering thorough the meadows, little pastoral figures and a lake with a big tower on the bank. Having no more orders of this kind he continued to paint landscapes for himself on wood, with hills and valleys, brooks meandering through the meadows, lakes with a big tower on the bank.

The question Menini posed to the long road where he lived also applies to the clear cut and tranquil landscapes which he wanted to continue to paint. One day he set it out in this way: 'I know that here there is a movement which can never stop when the sun is high because of business, and nothing can be motionless because the ebb and flow of the air is a great continual process of decay which we can also see with our eyes, seeing how the light confuses things rather than illuminating them. And the thicker the air is with the gas of that process of decay the less it leaves things in peace. Along with the light which distends them, along with the force of gravity which tires them by pulling at them from below, it causes them to decay continually without peace. But then I, Emanuele Menini, ask: What is this thought of immobility that comes into my head? Why do I have a desire to paint tranquil landscapes where clarity is peace? Is it because I am old and soft in the head?'

When the industrialist who made spiral staircases came back from his trip to the United States, where he had gone to find out how the real Californian villas are made, he talked to him for a long time about the air one breathes on the streets of Los Angeles. He told him that there too you can see very clearly the decaying air which you breathe, so that it is like here, and there is no difference. Menini's talk about the lack of ventilation in these plains, which makes everything unclear and shaky, seemed less unlikely to him. And on a visit to him in hospital he said to him: 'Menini, now I understand you better.'

At this time I wrote a letter to Menini from Birmingham telling him that, there too, there are suburbs and rootless people everywhere, and millions of people living in the suburbs scattered through the countryside. There too the light had become a strangely opaque filter and more visible than that which it ought to reveal outside of us, far off in the world.

Of all this Menini thought in the hospital: 'What can I do about it? I can't do anything. There is the movement which never stops. But to notice it one only has to look at the wave motion in the air. There is no need to take trips to America or England like this writer gentleman. Just look at the trees — are they going to take trips?'

In the autumn he had got into the habit of getting up very early. The first trucks had hardly begun to shake the glass in the windows as they went along the long street, than he rose and left the house to try to see the immobility of things in the dawn before the tremor arrived in the air and began the rush of every day.

During a walk we took in a park, in the month of November, he tried to tell me what he was looking for in the dawn. In the dawn he was trying to be in the company of the horizon, he was looking for a state of inner immobility — one which can only be found outside, in the space which opens out and breathes round something right up to the horizon.

Some mornings he got as far as the ring road which crosses the long street near his house, and from there on to a roundabout where cars and buses scattered in four directions. While the profile of the high buildings on the outskirts of town was swept by an uncertain light, the infrequent traffic between the big buildings of the four-lane highway looked like a liquid movement — there was as yet no bustle. Having reached the roundabout Menini waited for the rising of the sun, which came up over a mountain of rubbish which was visible at that point beyond a line of trees.

This is a mountain with a rectangular base and a track for the trucks running up along its slopes. When the peak of the mountain shone, a row of houses opposite, shaped like control towers, was directly struck by the rays of the sun and some of the windows had red gleams. Immediately after that radiant moment, the mountain of rubbish was extinguished, and Menini was sure he saw signs of something beginning out there where the skyscrapers on the outskirts had suddenly changed colour.

From the roundabout he hurried on to a park that stretches towards the line of hills — the one we were walking in that November afternoon when Menini explained the result of his researches to me. In that park, early in the morning, there was no one except young athletes running, old gentlemen taking a stroll after having gone to buy their paper, a couple of Somali women taking their masters' dogs for a walk. And none of them and no tree had a shadow because the rays of the sun, which were still very slanted, did not come over the hedge to the east which separates the park from the road.

Alongside the park there are big blocks of flats in the form of enormous cubes one on top of the other; and from them, early in the morning, Menini saw people come out and saw them make their way without shadows along the street still looking as if they were not busy. But scarcely had they reached the street, which was already touched by the rays of the sun, than they all acquired the outline of a shadow although it was still not solid on the asphalt.

Meantime the roofs of the cars began to shine, the leaves of the hedge had little gleams of light, the traffic became less fluid, moment by moment the number of people waiting for the bus increased. At this point Menini began to feel the tremor in the air, because the rush of every day had already begun.

And then, at this precise point in the day, he was able to think of a kind of immobility he had seen in the opaque light of dawn, and this thought kept alive his desire to paint limpid and tranquil landscapes.

'Why,' as he said during our walk, 'does one never see immobility? One thinks of it only after one has seen it, when the tremor is about to come over it and everything begins to move once more. But can I convince anyone that I have really seen immobility with my own eyes? No. I can only paint a landscape.'

After that walk in the month of November I never again met the landscape painter Emanuele Menini. Luciano and I often went looking for him in the usual bar and also at his house and at his workplace, but we never found him.

That winter was very hard — one of the hardest of the century. Towards Christmas there was a heavy snowfall on all the plains that the long road ran through, and on the following day the landscape painter Emanuele Menini was found dead in the snow in a ditch beside the road, near a telephone booth.

From that same telephone booth Menini had shortly before called the young industrialist who made spiral staircases to talk to him about something he had seen. He had said he had seen a little villa in the fields, close by, and that he had been able to have a good look at it because the air was very limpid after the snowfall and the snow brought out the outline of everything. He had also explained exactly where the place was.

The industrialist who made spiral staircases had got into his car at once thinking of Menini lost in that arctic cold and in a couple of hours had reached the place. He had found the landscape painter lying on his back in the snow and already dead.

He was buried in that cemetery in the suburbs in front of which he had once stopped to pray on his walk to the great cedar of Lebanon which had brought God to his mind. Apart from his three partners from the warehouse and four regulars from the usual bar, there was only the industrialist who made spiral staircases at the funeral.

His partners from the warehouse said that lately, because of the trouble with his lungs, he had always been in and out of hospital and that when he was out he spent his time on long walks for his researches. But that he should have walked in the deep snow to the place where he was found dead, sixty kilometres from home, seems rather odd.

It is also not very clear what had interested him about that little villa in the fields which he had said on the telephone he had had such a good look at.

In the spring the firm for which Luciano worked was called to replace the heating in the factory belonging to the industrialist who made spiral staircases. In this way Luciano saw the young industrialist again, talked to him often and got to know of an episode which I shall add to this brief account.

When he came back from the United States the industrialist had noticed that the woman he lived with was very interested in Menini's landscapes, as if they were the only thing that brought her a little peace. It was a very grey time for her, during which she often wept. A lawsuit against her millionaire husband who made tiles had not resolved anything, and she had been denied the custody of her little son.

The woman often sat motionless on a sofa looking at one of Menini's landscapes paying no attention to anyone. It seemed that this was her way of calming herself and not thinking any more about her misfortunes, of the hatred she felt for her husband, the tile millionaire. Evidently the limpid colours of these landscapes was beneficial — at least for her.

Some time before the industrialist had bought a huge estate which was an abandoned farm, about forty kilometres from the long road in the direction of the sea. And one day he had the idea of building a villa there with an adjoining park, and of installing turbines in the park to make wind. Turbines like this would have had to sweep the air clean, thus making external objects always clear cut and motionless and no longer tremulous.

In the estate of the big villa he had in mind to build, he also thought of planting a wood of Canadian chestnut trees and of stocking it with racoons. He also wanted to create watercourses which would flow in meanders among grasses and reeds. The winds produced by the turbines would have rippled the water and moved the grass in a fresh breeze highlighting, by contrast, the tranquil immobility of things round about.

All this would have produced the effect of living in a landscape by Menini. And there perhaps the woman he lived with — and whom he loved greatly — would have found peace.

When the industrialist proposed the project to Menini the latter had made only one objection — that if the turbines had been strong enough to sweep the air clean like the south wind, thus giving the impression that one was living in another world, they would however have produced a tremor no less than that on the long road.

In the end the fantastic project of the industrialist who made spiral staircases came to nothing. One day unexpectedly the woman he lived with had gone back to her husband, the tile millionaire, for no sensible reason that he was able to understand.

Latterly she had been indifferent to everything, and clearly she was not in the least interested in the artificial paradise he was planning.

In that vast piece of land, where he would have wished to live with the woman he loved, the industrialist had now had two hundred thousand poplars planted — trees which grow in haste and allow of notable profits.

To Luciano he had confessed to feeling very lonely in his big Californian villa, which moreover bore very little resemblance to the real Californian villas. A few days later he had left for Patagonia where he hoped to sell his spiral staircases.

Last summer Luciano Capelli and I wanted to visit the place where Emanuele Menini was found dead. We saw the telephone booth from which he had spoken and about three hundred metres from the long road the small house in which he must have noticed something that interested him for his researches.

It is a small house in a box-like style, standing alone in the middle of the fields, which one does not see very well from the road. To see it one has to go down a lane and stop in front of a hedge in which dog-roses are blooming. From there to the sea it is probably about twenty kilometres, but that landscape gives no hint of the crowds at the bathing resorts: it is quite empty. They grow tomatoes there, and further on in the middle of a field of wheat there rises the solitary tower of an electricity pylon.

The small house has a roof formed by four triangular gables and a square front with four windows, closed by rolling shutters of grey plastic which stand out against the indigo of the walls. Seen from a hundred metres or so away it looks very peaceful in the midst of the fields, with a television aerial flowering on the roof. Pots of flowers arranged near the door, a little garden wall from which there rises an ornamental laurel hedge, two little Arizona cypresses flanking the door complete its fine presence in that secluded spot.

The little house was mysterious — in itself it composed a world of images quite different from that of the via Emilia which passes nearby. The air was clean, the afternoon shade fell exactly between the two little cypresses which frame the door, recalling the feeling of a place permanently undisturbed like that of the avenues in cemeteries.

READERS OF BOOKS
ARE EVER MORE FALSE

A student of literature, who had come to Milan to read literature at the university, tried for a long time to understand what books mean and what the professors mean when they speak about books and literature.

The moment he set foot in the university he had at once begun to feel uncomfortable, because all the talk he heard during lectures was incomprehensible to him. Moreover he was ashamed to come from a technical college — whose students are considered inferior to those who come from high schools — and so our student often blushed.

Sometimes, not understanding even a tenth of the sentences of one of his teachers, he blushed up to his ears and had to escape from the lecture hall. He looked everywhere for a book that might explain to him what books and professors mean.

One day he got to know four Neapolitan students and noticed that, thanks to their long experience as students who had failed and were now extramural, they had got to the point of forming some ideas about what happens in university lecture halls. Our student had not yet managed to find a book that might explain to him what books and professors mean, so he turned to the four Neapolitan students who very willingly undertook to explain to him the ideas they had formed on the subject.

They explained to him that in the university lecture halls every teacher merely boasted about having thoroughly understood the books he has read, and that the students have only to learn to do the same.

Our student then began to observe all his professors closely and in the end the explanation seemed convincing to him. So he set about learning his teachers' way of talking, and their attitudes, in order to be able to boast that he too had thoroughly understood the books in the syllabus and thus to pass some exams.

To begin with the matter seemed a little difficult because of all the books in the syllabus he ought to read, but then the four Neapolitan students came to his help explaining to him what to do. They explained that it was enough to extract from a book some striking sentences, so as to be able to set one idea against another and thus demonstrate that he had understood everything. In fact, according to them, you didn't even have to extract the striking sentences from the book, but from the introduction which explains what the book is about, and this was the best method.

Putting this advice into practice, the student of literature did indeed pass some exams with good marks. But at this point he felt a doubt arise and he mulled over it for some months with his head in a state of confusion. The doubt was this: while it was now very clear to him that the professors do not talk to boast about what is written in the book but merely to boast about themselves for having understood it, for the same reason it was not at all clear to him what was written in books and so what he himself was saying when in an exam he boasted of having understood them.

Stymied by this thought he wandered through the streets thinking about it, and not thinking any more about the exams he should have sat. One day he at last found the courage to set out his problem to the four Neapolitans in these words: 'In short, if the professors merely talk about what they have understood, what do the books talk about?'

The four replied cheerfully that they had no idea, and all the other students to whom he posed the problem gave him the same answer as did two assistant lecturers, somewhat taken aback by such a question. But to him the question seemed plausible and then our student began once more to feel ashamed and to blush, not only because he didn't understand but because the others made fun of his attempts to understand.

His situation as a student became more and more impossible. With doubts of this kind in his head and seeing that all this made no sense to the others, he resolved to leave the university and to break off any relations with the groups of students with whom he lived, for whom books were merely something one had to pretend to have understood, pretending to have understood what the professors had understood so as to pass the exams.

He decided to find a job where he could give himself over to the reading of a great number of books on his own (without having to listen to the boasts of the professors), so as finally to determine what they talked about and what they meant.

The long road that leads to the outskirts of a metropolis is often depressing but almost always easy to go along — the buses leave every minute. Taking one of these buses our student of literature managed to find cheap lodgings in a district at the furthest limits of the inhabited world. Here he immediately began to read lots of books which he had collected in an attempt to understand what they meant and so find his way in life.

The tiny flat in which he installed himself he shared with a young woman with no profession, who like him had little money to spend. This woman, too, had travelled along the long road to the outskirts after leaving her husband and therewith the profession of wife, the only profession she had.

This remote district seemed to be depopulated, without shops, with dogs wandering in the streets and very few cars going about. On the ground there was always a thin reddish mud and in the air a kind of wandering cloud of dust, as if the wind carried the desert sand there. But that was only because of excavations to extend the water and gas mains to the new apartment blocks that were rising.

From their windows the two saw only the windows of other houses like the one they lived in, or else carcasses of cars reduced to a rusty mess in a vast wasteland fought over by metal junk and fast-spreading weeds. But on misty days they finally could no longer see anything — everything disappeared as far as the horizon, and then the two knew only that they were there, living in a big block, in the vast world in which they too had turned up like the rainworms in the earth.

The house was always untidy, the one lying on the divan in the living room reading books from morning to night, the other sitting in the kitchenette chewing gum and leafing through piles of magazines: that is how the student of literature and the young woman without a profession passed much of their days until it was supper time. They hardly ever went out, having little money to spend, but every so often they listened to the noises of the external world, noticing that it was raining outside, that summer was over, that there was fog, that it was far into autumn.

In the evening they went to bed early, slept a lot and had very long dreams. For both of them sleeping was so easy, the easiest thing in the world.

Some evenings the student turned up muttering in the young woman's room, impelled by youthful ardour to mount her. And she received him in her bed or not according to how she was feeling that day.

In the grey autumn afternoons the young woman sometimes got tired of leafing through magazines and chewing gum alone in the kitchen, and went to sit in the living room to watch the student reading books. She was very curious about this activity of reading books, partly because she herself never managed to read a page full of words without getting tired; she was always left confused by these lines all printed the same which gave her a feeling of boredom and discouraged her from reading.

When she went into the living room to watch the student reading, she sat for a long time in silence but in the end she always had the need to know: 'Is it fun to read so much?' Then he laid down the book and began to talk to her about novels and famous novelists, about poets and playwrights, and even about some thinkers whose ideas at once made his listener drop off to sleep.

Every day she went through the jobs vacant in the paper, underlining the more interesting ones and proposing to herself to telephone the next day to find out what exactly it entailed. But after supper she forgot everything including the jobs vacant, went to bed early, and had very long dreams.

But the moment came when the two fellow-lodgers had hardly any money left, they had to make up their minds to earn some. The young woman managed with a modest loan from a sister who lived in Codogno, and the student had now been living too long on what was left of a grant, while he waited to find his way in life.

The student thought that the best thing for him would be to go and sell books, in this way he would be able to continue to read a lot. Perhaps he would be able to speak about what he read to customers and get advice from anyone who had read more than he — that was his lively hope.

A middle-aged man with a moustache received them in the office of a big publishing house that dealt with sales by instalments, and explained that it was a question of selling books on the instalment plan from house to house — encyclopedias above all. The man with the moustache quickly revealed that he was the head of the office — an engineer who had taken to selling books because this job allowed him to make a lot of money, as he himself very frankly admitted.

'I have a sure way of selling and about that there is no doubt,' said the man with the moustache, 'but it's a question of seeing whether a person has the qualities to understand it. I shall take you round though to let you see how one does it and then we'll decide.'

It is a windy day — it is drizzling. In the engineer's big car the student and the young woman go round districts on the outskirts of the town which they did not even know existed — districts with high buildings rising in the midst of barren landscapes or districts that seem to be infinite expanses of posters or else areas crossed by floods of vehicles that are flowing towards some freeway. They have with them lists of possible customers furnished by the sales department of the big publishing house and they leaf through them, looking out of the car windows, wondering where they are and what will happen.

All day long the same things happen. They go and ring the bell of a possible buyer in one of those big buildings and present themselves to strangers, saying they are doing market research — they would like to interview someone from the family to know what his favourite reading is, what he would like to read etc.

The engineer has already explained to his two pupils that this phase of the approach to the client must not last more than three minutes from the minute the bell is rung. In three minutes the salesman must manage to get invited into the house, sit down comfortably, carry out the interview writing the replies on an appropriate form, and immediately propose to the interviewee the purchase of an encyclopedia or a series of very expensive volumes; then while he is explaining the system of monthly instalments, he must already be drawing up the sales contract.

The two pupils watch the engineer move about at ease in the houses of those strangers whose bell they have rung. They watch those strangers, disoriented in their own homes, in their living rooms, among their furniture and ornaments, while they are being persuaded to buy very expensive books that they have never heard of and which do not interest them.

But if the strangers shake their heads to say that the matter doesn't interest them, the engineer immediately quotes their answers which are written on the form, showing that they are contradicting themselves.

If the strangers then make more substantial objections, as for example, 'No, I do not buy books, I have plenty of other things to think about,' the engineer replies brusquely and without looking them in the face, clearly showing that they are making him lose precious time. And he systematically interrupts their objections, giving the whole list of valid reasons for buying books.

The two pupils see that the engineer's skill consists in replying confidently to all the objections, citing the reasons for buying, and so in dealing speedily with their objections (this phase must not last more than six minutes), immediately offering the client his pen to sign the contract.

As the engineer has already explained to the two pupils, the salesman must always sit down on the right of the client, so that the gesture of putting the pen in his hand appears more simple and the signing of the contract results as the outcome of a natural dynamic. And this is a movement of great skill which each time surprises the two pupils.

Finding himself with his pen in his hand and not managing to bring to mind other objections, the client lowers his fist and signs the contract, which is immediately snatched from his hand by the engineer, who is already standing up and ready to make for the door. Sometimes while the engineer is leaving the stranger repents of having signed and calls him back to discuss the matter. Without turning round the engineer replies that he will have to sort it out with the lawyers of the publishing house because a contract is a contract and must be respected.

Other times, at the door it happens that the stranger wants to know something about the books he has bought. Then the engineer replies drily that he knows nothing about them because he only sells books and wouldn't dream of reading them.

Before sending them off to sell books in some remote suburb the engineer furnished the two pupils with very precise instructions concerning the spirit of his method. In particular he said: 'Never give the client confidence. The client must always be kept a little at a disadvantage, a bit intimidated, in that way he buys in a hurry to get rid of his embarrassment. But if you treat him well, he thinks he is clever and doesn't buy anything. Watch out — that is the way of the world.'

Now let us imagine the student of literature and the young woman sent out on a sales mission. The student presents himself in the houses of strangers with the confident talk and style of a man without scruples, in imitation of the engineer. The young woman acts as his assistant, handing out the form for the interview, the contract and the pen at the right moment.

When it is the moment to demolish the objections of the strangers, the student keeps to the spirit of the method. And the spirit of the method says that one must always answer the objections of customers with phrases that have nothing to do with those objections, but which suggest a valid reason for buying. Only thus at a certain point will the client lose the thread of his thoughts and no other objections will come to his mind.

But if it is very easy to demolish the objections, to get the pen into the client's right hand in such a natural way that he signs the contract almost without noticing, this is a move of great skill, which is rather difficult to acquire.

For this reason after six days of hard work — during which they went round depressing districts from morning to evening, always trying that move with the pen and never bringing it off — the couple have not yet managed to sell a book.

The engineer sent for them and asks them: 'Tell me — what is wrong with you two? Are you not right in the head? Do you drink? Or are you people who read books?'

The student admits, hanging his head, that he is a person who reads books — a lot of them. Whereupon the engineer begins to shout furiously: 'That's why you sell nothing, Jesus! The customers smell you out.'

Then he calms down and sets out for the two pupils the reality of things: 'A customer buys because he is uncomfortable or intimidated — in short, put at a disadvantage and only for that reason. But if he gets a hint that the salesman is someone who reads books, he gets suspicious. He becomes suspicious that he will have to read the books as well as buy them. And then he won't buy anything — he is a customer ruined for life.'

The engineer adds in a worried tone: 'Because the customers get a whiff of things. Jesus, they get a whiff! That is why a good salesman must never read books so that he doesn't give them a whiff of himself and thus put the customer on his guard.'

The student of literature did not grasp this idea properly, because he did not attach too much importance to it so as not to have to make an effort to understand things that don't interest him; basically he is interested in reading books, he is not interested in whether the customers smell him out.

More days go past when the pen for signing the contract never manages to get into the right hand of the customer with the desired naturalness, because the customer protests in a lively way when it is thrust into his hand by force and sometimes throws out the two intruders, who find themselves in the street depressed and bewildered.

The engineer sent for them again to deliver an ultimatum: 'Listen to me, you two, and for the last time because I don't have time to lose. You must ask yourselves this: What is a book? A book is printed paper to sell rather than something to read. This is the reality of things. If you understand this you have in your hand a key thought and you will be able to free yourselves of all illusions about books.'

The engineer continues: 'And note that the customer sees things in the same way. He too only wants the reality of things not the illusions of words. Only when you have transformed yourselves, becoming like him, will he be able to see you as people like himself. Because at last he will no longer get a whiff of the illusions which fill the heads of readers of books. Do you agree to change? You have ten days to show it.'

The student hastily muttered that he agreed to change but only because he was so confused that he didn't know what he was saying. On the other hand, to go about for six days of the week in unknown parts of the world eating sandwiches in bars and getting home only late in the evening, tired and stupefied — is not this in itself a great change of life? And when is there ever time left to think about the books to be read?

But Sunday comes. Alone at home all day the student finds it natural to take up a novel and read it until the evening, losing himself in the illusions and daydreams of which books speak.

In the evening the young woman comes back from a visit to her sister who lives in Codogno, and finds her fellow-lodger deep in reading. She says to him: 'But why don't you really stop reading books as the engineer said?'

The student replies: 'It's all madness — the theory of a madman — do you believe it?'

The young woman explains: 'But we have to earn money — we have no choice.'

And the student, throwing the book to the ground, shouts very annoyed: 'It's very easy for you who only read magazines to come and lecture me about books. Why don't you go alone and sell the encyclopedias? You are so ignorant, the customers certainly won't smell you out.'

The young woman thought the student had a point. Since she had never read books, if she turned up alone she would not be smelt out by the customers.

So she went back to being a woman with a profession — she cut her hair short with a fringe, she altered an old skirt, shortening it to the knees, she put on lipstick and high heels (she was somewhat small), and one fine morning she went out alone to sell books from house to house in the outskirts of the town. There she is waiting for a bus along with other people in broad daylight.

Two weeks later. One evening the student came home livid in the face because not even that day did he sell anything. The woman prepared supper and the two sat at table. The student asks: 'Tell me, how did you get on today?' She answers: 'Two encyclopedias today too.'

After supper the student stands there staring at the wall and talking to himself: 'I too would like to be accepted by the customers as one of them. I'd like to change, to really transform myself, but I can't manage. I am so ashamed.'

The woman says: 'If you like I'll help.' He asks: 'But how?' She thinks about it and replies: 'I would see you didn't fall into temptation.'

We are in the month of November and the young woman's business is booming. Now the engineer was very satisfied with the couple who had really changed. He didn't know that they went to work separately — every evening two or three contracts arrived on his desk and that is what counts. Meantime the student never sold anything and lived off the young woman.

Coming back from work, she kept watch on him silently to see whether he was still thinking about books to read. She followed him from one room to another so that he would not fall into the temptation of taking up a book. Every so often she tried to understand what was going on in his mind suddenly saying to him: 'Confess that you are still thinking of books to read.'

Almost always he took refuge in remaining silent, but at other times he confessed blushing: 'Yes, it's true — I still think about them.' Then she gave him advice: 'Why don't you try looking through my magazines when you are tempted?'

On Sundays she went to Codogno to her sister's to take a walk in the country and had to take him with her, otherwise being alone in the house he would surely have started to read a book. But the student did not like these walks much — he was bored when she pointed out the country smells and above all he couldn't stand her sister who only talked about her children and things for the house. In short, these Sunday trips to the country made him more irritated than the workdays.

On workdays ever since he could no longer read books, nor even think about what they meant, the student was always very agitated. He was in a state of desperation which nothing got him out of, except the thought of mounting a woman.

So every night the young woman took him into her bed. And there before falling asleep, he began to talk to her about a strange thought which constantly assailed him; 'Is it really me who is living this life? It doesn't feel like it to me, because it is too stupid. That is — I feel as if it is not me but someone else whom I watch from outside, and I know all about him and am ashamed for him. But if I see this other person from the outside where am I? Am I something or nothing?'

Over and above this every night he woke up with insomnia (the time is over when to sleep was so easy) and he had to go into the kitchen and look at a wall, waiting for sleep to come back.

Then the young woman got up too to see that he didn't start reading a book on the sly. And finding him sitting with his head in his hands being sorry for himself, she took pity on him. She brought him a few magazines to leaf through and offered him a stick of gum to chew to distract him from his thoughts and from the temptations.

In spite of all the efforts of his fellow-lodger, the student in fact actually went in search of temptations. For example he stopped to look in the window of every bookshop he found in his path.

One morning in front of a bookshop he met a university lecturer whom he used to stop and talk to sometimes. The other invited him to a conference to be held in a theatre at the civic centre, where there would be famous critics and writers, and the student accepted the invitation.

When Sunday came he pretended to be ill so as not to go with the young woman to Codogno. In the afternoon he took a bus and went to an old theatre full of hundreds upon hundreds of readers of books. Here a famous critic with a very distinguished and very youthful air was talking, and immediately after him another famous critic with a more mature look, whom everyone called Aborgast (the name of a character in a Hitchcock film whom he did not resemble at all).

The student of literature listened to these speeches with his heart beating hard, among other things because he did not understand very much. But when the public was invited to ask questions, he raised his hand and found the strength to address the critic called Aborgast, in order to question him about his literary tastes.

Aborgast replied like this: 'My literary tastes? I want a book not to be whining. If a writer is desperate let him hang himself. I read two or three pages and if I find them whining or desperate I give it a bad review. There is nothing better than a really bad review to warn the author that he is taking the wrong road.'

Disconcerted by this speech and feeling very ashamed, the student nevertheless found the courage to ask another question which he had been nursing for a long time, about what books mean. But this annoyed Aborgast very much and he interrupted the discussion saying: 'These are things one asks only if one understands nothing about literature. If I find this question in a book I finish the writer off for life.'

More depressed than ever the student went home blushing up to his ears and shaking with shame, because the replies of that famous critic had made him feel stupid and very ignorant. And he had no sooner got home than he at once began to read a book while waiting for his companion to return from Codogno.

The next day he began to read books secretly, whenever he could, above all when going about in buses or on the metro. Arriving in front of a high building where he had to interview a customer to persuade him to buy an encyclopedia, he lost the desire to do so every time and went to find a bar where he could get on with his reading. At the end of his supposed work some evenings he stopped in a milk-bar below his flat to finish a novel begun in the morning and then threw it in the dustbin before going home.

By now he had no more desire to go around in depressing districts aimlessly reading novelettes bought at station stalls. He no longer felt like being a salesman of books on the instalment plan. He dreamt of being a writer — of becoming a critic and publishing books that others would go and sell with success. So he stopped altogether going in to those depressing districts and now only wandered about in the big city — dreaming and wandering, wandering and dreaming all day long.

One night he was taken by the strong urge to mount the young woman several times. When he at last felt satisfied the following sentences came from his mouth: 'How nice it would be to be able to read a novel until the dawn. Then to have a shower, sit down at one's typewriter and write an article explaining what that book means. I have come to see that this is my way through life.'

Fantasies like this seemed somewhat bizarre to the young woman who began to laugh. He was offended and went back to his room banging the door. Next day he began to read books openly.

By now winter was coming and the student spent the whole day in the streets of the city centre going into every bookshop and planning to buy books of every kind on a colossal scale. The replies of that famous critic called Aborgast — the one who had made him feel stupid and very ignorant — were still burning and he was pondering forms of revenge.

He went to the engineer to tell him that he was resigning and that his method was a complete fraud. The engineer with the moustache almost thumped him one.

Some people think that ambitions are prejudices which try to acquire substance through our anguish. And at this moment the student had many forms of anguish because he aimed to take his leave of that other person who led a ridiculous and stupid life — that other person whom he looked at from the outside and of whom he was ashamed, who certainly was not him but someone else, a poor thing, who knows who.

After having been thrown out and insulted by the engineer he was no sooner on the street than he could no longer bear the idea of sharing the flat with that little woman who was so sure of herself and who understood nothing of his ambitions.

He went off to live with a girl who to begin with had pretended to him that she was a great reader of novels, passionately fond of all kinds of literature, but who then turned out to be merely a liar — someone who had read a few books because she had to at school, and after that she hadn't managed to read any more because (as she confessed) any book threw her into an immediate deep sleep.

The discovery greatly disappointed our student of literature. But since he was already installed in the liar's house, and it was a hard winter and the house was comfortable, he thought it better to stay there.

In the month of May the engineer started looking at the young woman with the eyes of a man who is fascinated. Not only did she bring him good contracts every day but she was also able to look after the organisation of the office and had moreover found a way to review and extend the list of possible customers. Since this work was greatly appreciated by a director of the big publishing house, the woman was offered a job in head office.

So she stopped working for the engineer with the moustache and one May evening the engineer invited her to dinner to say goodbye to her.

They had no sooner sat down at table in a country inn near the Ticino river than the engineer became aware that the young woman's eyes were fascinating him — to the point of making him stammer.

Someone at a nearby table was telling how the month before a decomposed corpse had arrived here, washed ashore under the cement pier, and it had been that of a man who had had a heart attack while fishing. This not very cheerful conversation had impelled the mature engineer to try his luck, thinking it was something the corpse couldn't do.

He therefore took courage to pay court to the woman with the very beautiful eyes, and did so all evening, asking her at the end to run off with him.

'Run off where?' asked the woman laughing.

'I'll take you to see Bangkok, Singapore, Bali,' the man proposed, 'wouldn't you like to take a nice trip?'

'No. I prefer to go to my sister's in Codogno,' the woman replied adding serenely: 'I am telling you right away — you have no hope with me.'

Did the engineer weigh these replies well during the evening and the days that followed? That we don't know. But the fact is that now the sun of his desire rises early in the morning and sets only when night has fallen, lighting up his eyes with strange little flashes.

The engineer with the moustache is unsettled; he neglects his business and finally goes to a tourist agency to get tickets for a trip to Bangkok, Singapore, Bali. He sends them to the young woman, and gets them back by return of post with a little message: 'I prefer to go to Codogno.'

At this point we can perhaps imagine the thoughts that come to the mind of the man with the moustache. He is thinking of that woman who arrived in his office six months ago, an awkward and defenceless reader of books (like that wretched partner of hers, the student) and who then transformed herself into a magnificent saleswoman whom no customer can any longer smell out. But in this woman there is something else, which the engineer cannot grasp and which keeps him in suspense — above all her magnificent eyes.

One evening he goes and rings her bell after dinner because he had a need to talk to her. The moment the young woman opens the door he immediately confesses to her the admiration he feels for her beautiful eyes, from which he feels he understands something she carries within her.

'That comes from the fact that I am short-sighted,' the woman explains. 'I have a slight squint.'

'It doesn't matter,' exclaims the man, beside himself, 'I have an ulcer.'

And he throws himself on her for an embrace, but she runs away from him in the shadows of the corridor. Pursuing her, the engineer reaches the living room where he stops with staring eyes like someone greatly surprised.

The shelves of a library are packed with books and on the table and on the chairs other books are scattered as if kept within reach. On the arm of an easy chair under a lamp a big volume is open with a bookmark.

The engineer takes up the book and sees that it is a famous French novel. It is a title in the catalogue of another publishing house — one reserved for people who really read and whom he despises because they only manage to scrape together contracts worth a few cents.

The engineer comments: 'Books for refined people, for people who really read books and then take credit for it. You were reading, weren't you?'

The woman nods and the man goes on: 'So you never stopped reading books. You did not change as you made me believe. You made fun of me and of my method it seems.'

The woman declares she has never read a whole book in her life but when her companion went off she became curious to know what he found so passionately interesting in books. She bought these books but cannot manage to read them.

The engineer sways in the middle of the room making gestures of sadness: 'A pitiful lie! You don't want to offend me and I thank you for it, thank you from my heart. But I see that you don't want to have anything to do with me because I don't read your books.'

He is thoughtful for a moment and then goes on: 'Yes, I don't read your books and my head isn't full of all that stuff you find in books — illusions nothing but illusions. I have within me different things — maybe healthier ones.'

He lowers his voice and murmurs: 'You will never be able to take me for someone like yourself, as my customers do. I and my customers, we recognise each other frankly and they don't smell me out. But you readers of books smell everyone out because what you read deludes you and makes you proud. I am simple and crude compared to you — I know that.'

The woman says in a very tired voice: 'Please go away because I am sleepy.'

The man at once turns round, makes for the door, goes down the stairs, gets into his car, and finally loses himself in the district where the blocks of flats are identical and the street lights seem to be there only to make one melancholy.

In the long months of solitude the young woman had discovered that after all one can even manage to read books. She would never have been able to read an entire book — but a few pages, maybe a few chapters, yes.

In the empty winter evenings in that completely silent house the temptation to take up a book and begin to read it had begun to emerge in her too. Little by little she had learned that the lines of print — all of them the same — which had always put her off reading by their boring uniformity, could make voices come into her mind.

In this way the words in the books began to assume different tones, to recall serious or jocular persons who speak in hints and strange turns of phrase, and the lines of print ceased to be all the same.

At the end of winter, however, she noticed that the words and sentences she read in books — just because they made voices come into her mind — made an impression on her like ghost films.

Listening to all these allusions and insinuations about people and places and events and feelings, she began to have a feeling that she could not control and which put her on her guard about everything. They were like voices which emerged from a door opened on to the darkness. Alone in the house she listened to every slightest noise and peered at every shadow which looked a little unusual to her, because the words in a book had brought this trepidation upon her.

Therefore she could never get on with her reading — not because a book seemed not very fascinating, but on the contrary because the individual words and sentences were too fascinating for her, awoke too many questions which she could not shake off.

After reading a page or two she sat for a long time on the armchair in the living room chewing gum with the book open on her knees but without looking at it. She tried to control the influence that the words had on her — one made up of thousands of questions which swarmed on the page, because of those hints and winks which emerged like a lure.

Over these months she had bought a lot of books, trying to find one in which the words would make less impression on her and thus allow her to read on. But that did not seem to be possible — either she cast her eyes on books that at once bored her because she felt no trepidation, or else she immediately felt that trepidation which fascinated her at each word and sentence and did not allow her to go on.

This is the point she had come to in her research to establish what is exciting in books, when at the beginning of the summer various events came to interrupt her.

One day the engineer went and waited for her in front of the building where she worked, came up to her and said without any preamble: 'I have read the book you were reading and I didn't dislike it, I have to say. Let's meet and talk about it because I want to ask you about further reading as well. I'd like to read a lot.'

She replied that she had never read a whole book in her life and had nothing to tell him.

He tried to detain her whispering: 'Come on, Signorina Virginia, throw off your mask with me once and for all. Listen — I am ready to go over to your side. I no longer care that my customers should take me for one of them or that they should smell me out.'

By running into the nearby street she got away from other speeches, and for a time had no more news of the engineer. Then at the beginning of July the student of literature got in touch again, beginning by telephoning her very often to tell her about himself.

For some months the student had been back in the city he came from, some seventy kilometres from Milan. He had inherited a little money and now wrote and read and did nothing else as he had long desired. He had also joined a select workshop of aspiring writers, directed by that distinguished critic with the youthful air whom he had once heard talk along with Aborgast; so now one evening a week he came to Milan to take part in the meetings of the workshop.

On the phone the student told the woman everything that happened concerning the progress of his career among the aspiring writers. He talked to her about their discussions, about a review they were going to start, about the articles he intended to write to demonstrate something, to put someone down, or to demolish some current mystification.

The woman on the telephone listened to him in silence. She had now adopted the habit of talking to herself when she was at home and during these telephone calls she often felt like talking to herself for fun, putting her hand over the receiver and thus letting the student talk as long as he liked.

But one evening he mentioned something which caught her attention like a bell, although she was not concentrating. She asked him to repeat what he had said and the student repeated it: during the last meeting of the group of aspiring writers, he had suddenly turned round and whom had he seen sitting at the back of the room? The engineer with the moustache — yes, the very man, listening to their debate about a best-selling novel.

What the engineer with the moustache was doing at these meetings we don't know. But for several weeks he reappeared, sitting in the shadow at the back of the room, listening to their discussions of best-sellers. That is what the student of literature told her on the phone; he found that presence somewhat embarrassing as well as mysterious.

In August the city emptied; the district was more deserted than ever apart from dogs straying or lying on the pavements. It was the holiday season and one evening the student proposed that the young woman come to the sea with him. Would she like to spend a week by the sea? Very well, he would come and fetch her in a car next day at ten. He had so many things to tell her!

Next day, long before the agreed time, the young woman went to the station and took a train for Codogno where she then stayed for the whole of her holidays.

At Codogno she was alone — her sister's family were at the sea. Every evening she listened to the words of a book and it seemed to her that with the windows open their effect on her was different.

She succeeded in giving in to these moments of trepidation; she no longer resisted the feelings of danger. She stopped chewing gum; then she would hear voices speaking to her in silence, feel the immense night around her, while her body was as firmly set in the world as the armchair in which she sat. A state of abandon would come over her like a promise and plunge her into sleep.

At the beginning of October the first issue of the review for aspiring writers finally appeared, edited by the critic with the youthful air. The student of literature published an article in it and his article immediately acquired a certain notoriety for the summary way in which he dismissed many books, some films and other things. It was also quoted in a national daily as a good example of sarcastic but incoherent prose (the excessive number of anacoluthons was noticeable).

One Sunday the student turned up at the young woman's door, showing her the review with his article and the paper that talked about him — and the woman had to listen to him for six hours.

First of all he told her what had happened at his workshop's last meeting during a discussion on a recent best-selling novel. The engineer with the moustache was sitting as usual in the shadow at the back of the room, and at a certain point had got up and shouted in a broken voice: 'Enough! Enough! It's too much!' Staggering and with a distraught air he had made for the door. No one had understood what he meant by that shout; he seemed mad.

After this story the student had begun to talk about the moments of progress in his literary career. He had learned that in this business one had to put oneself in the limelight and take part in a lot of conferences and he had already taken part in eight conferences with critics and famous writers. He had also put himself in the limelight with the article in the review and had already written another one which would attract even more attention than the first because of the excellent demolition pieces it contained.

He explained that that too was a good way to get on — and in fact there was a critic called Aborgast who had become famous for his articles which were full of dismissive pieces. He was very pleased with his new article because here, in the space of a few pages, he had managed to dismiss five famous novels, three highly successful films, as well as Goethe, a celebrated rock singer and two American astronauts.

It was an hour since the young woman had stopped listening to him and had begun to talk to herself as a distraction. During supper the student held forth on the strange behaviour of the engineer, who had perhaps gone mad and certainly was very unpleasant and ill-mannered. But she was no longer listening to him because she was intent on talking to herself.

Suddenly the student asked: 'But what are you doing — are you mumbling to yourself?'

And she continued aloud the reflection she was making on the words in books: 'It's like when we are children and certain words mean something or other to us. Or certain streets, a house, even a shadow, may mean something or other to us. May it not be that all these things cause trepidation precisely because they are nothing at all?'

The student asked with some annoyance: 'What, they are nothing? What has come into your head?'

The young woman explained: 'They are impressions that disappear from one moment to the next, and afterwards you no longer know what they are.'

Rising to his feet the student replied to her: 'May one know what you are getting at talking like this? What does all you have said prove? Why don't you make up your mind to read something serious for once?'

He grabbed his briefcase and his article and, still very annoyed, ran off to catch a train.

At the end of October the woman had found a place to live which was not in the suburbs, but the flat wasn't ready yet and she was going to have to wait a month before getting into it. Meantime with the first rains of autumn the engineer popped up again and came to meet her as she left work. This will be their last meeting.

Now we see them right in the middle of a huge square in the shadow of three buildings forming parallelepipeds against the sky, on which an infinite number of little non-opening windows make up the smooth and polished surface of the looming walls. The man with the moustache comes up to the woman and whispers with a wary air: 'I want to come over to your side. You must hear what I have to tell you about that book I read. I have read it three times already. I absolutely must speak to you.'

The woman points out to him: 'I can't stand you any more — understand that.'

The man is astounded and after a pause begins to say: 'I am used to speaking clearly to my customers because I know they are simple people and not false.'

The woman interrupts him: 'If you come looking for me again I shall phone your wife.'

But the engineer goes on under the looming buildings with their unopenable windows: 'You readers of books really are strange! Goodness knows who you all think you are! You hide behind reserve because you are incapable of accepting anyone, or else you speak without speaking to anyone. I have also noticed that you rarely look another person in the eye. Signorina Virginia, why?'

This last question is addressed to Signorina Virginia who is already far off in the vast square, but she does not hear it and it is as if the man had not said anything.

Already far away, she was mulling over all these requests for attention which the student and the man with the moustache are always making of her and began to talk to herself.

An hour later she was walking along a street full of shop windows and noticed that even the words in the advertisements, on the walls, on the posters, in the shops, kept asking for her attention. It felt as if they were all winking to her, but in a different way from the ones in books, because they did not cause her trepidation. They were there only to say: 'You understand me, eh?'

Even watching people's movements she thought she saw something. The glances that were exchanged, the kind of gait they assumed, the way they turned round looking for something in the shop windows — all those were movements to say the same thing. They all said: 'You understand who I am, eh?'

All this talk going on around her with movements and winks was no different from the way she spoke to herself except that it was on a larger scale. This street was like a huge mind in which words and thoughts of shadows wandered, but where the shadows going about seemed to be ashamed to be shadows, and then kept making requests for attention in order not to be taken for shadows. And everybody took everybody else for something else.

Those shadows that were ashamed to be shadows crowded together in a tiny space, a street, surrounded with immense spaces which vanished into infinity. And in that space there was in the air a kind of dust which found its way into every corner, covered all the shadows and objects, deposited itself on the neon lights and the shop windows. It was a strange kind of dust, which made whatever it touched stupid and which nothing could stop — because dust naturally gets into every corner.

In her vision the young woman had the thought that the dust was part of the soil, was just the heavy quality of the earth, raised by the wind to form a cloud which wrapped the shadows in burdensome stupidity — or the dull stupor of being mere shadows.

Then why all these requests for attention which the shadows made as they wandered about? Why all that winking without trepidation in their movements and words?

At this point she realised that the passers-by were turning to look at her, because she was talking to herself out loud. She felt embarrassed, but suddenly it didn't bother her any more because what was in her mind was: 'Well, maybe everything that happens is a mistake.'

One morning in the office she heard that the engineer with the moustache was dead. Driving at top speed he had had a collision at a crossroads at Lambrate. In the office her colleagues said that recently the engineer had been greatly changed, he neglected his business, he had also begun to read books and bored everyone by wanting to talk about them. Poor thing, he had been such a good salesman and office manager. Who knew what had happened to him.

As soon as she got home the woman began to get rid of all her books, carrying them into the street and leaving them in front of a rubbish bin. She made various trips in the lift, up and down in the building, which seemed to be empty, and by midnight had freed herself of all the printed paper she had in the house.

From the time when the words and sentences in books no longer disturbed her like ghost films, because she had learned to give in to the moments of trepidation, she seemed to see in these little black marks something even more disquieting.

Just as happened to her with the writing in the street and the posters fleetingly seen, so she thought she made out in the printed lines something uncertain and indistinct — like a mute apparition against which the words moved restlessly.

It seemed to her that written words and words in general were constantly emitting signals to attract attention with the strangest kind of winks. They were winking to her as if to say: 'Listen because now we are going to tell you something,' without then saying anything. They were only standing in the way of a strange apparition, which lacked the power of speech and which was emerging out there.

Once it occurred to her that all the sentences in the books and newspapers and posters had only this aim: to prevent this mute apparition from appearing and to keep away the embarrassment which the thought of it might have caused.

In the lift in the morning, going up to the office, she found herself face to face with persons she knew or did not know. There too, when the mute apparition began to emerge in a second's silence or in the casual glances exchanged, suddenly phrases rushed up to bar the way to that threat: 'How are you?' 'It's hot today.' 'Did you see the match on TV?'

In the office she stopped to watch men and women talking, and noticed how they always moved their hands and arms to show that they were talking. What were they saying? Always things the others knew already. But it seemed that for everyone it was very important to utter words and sentences to show that they wanted to say something, only to say nothing or call the attention of others to the fact that they were talking. Sometimes the people she watched pretended to express surprise, and some indicated there was nothing to be surprised about. At other times they pretended to express sorrow, and some went through the motions of being interested in sorrow. They were always intent on showing that they were expressing something so as to block off any mute apparition.

Now, as she talked to herself in the distant outskirts of the town, it seemed to her that books had led her to have too many ideas and that each fit of trepidation put other ideas into her head, and that it was a misfortune to have so many ideas in one's head.

Now in the office she could see nothing but this exchange of phrases, the endless performance to silence embarrassing thought and to ward off the apparition out there. Then to calm herself she began to chew a stick of gum with alacrity and said to herself: 'They are the others.' And thought as well: 'I wonder what film *they* are in.'

At the end of November she moved into an empty apartment that had been redecorated, where there was not a single book and nothing to remind her of that performance she saw in other people. And yet the strange thing was there, in the silent surface of the walls, in the mauve-painted windows, or in the oddly obtuse angles of the corridor. She had to talk to herself and try to be happy confronted by that mute apparition which watched her out there all the time.

Only an old streetlight in the park opposite comforted her when it went on at sunset, greeting her with a magnanimous gesture: 'Hello! We're here this evening too.'

In January she had to take part in a press conference called by her publishing house at which the publication of a series of new novels with huge print runs was announced. In the room were sitting lecturers, critics and writers, journalists and the heads of the publishing house, and a few aspiring writers whose novels were about to be presented to the press.

After the formal introductions, a young expert from the publishing house said: 'It is a moment of expansion in the market and we have to think of new initiatives that keep up with the times. In the sector of the novel an emphasis on everyday speech and the culture of crisis no longer convince anyone. Instead there is a need to return to methods that will enable more extensive communication and in this process of reclamation to come down on the side of the feelings. Because we are very aware of what people are feeling, we know what people want to read and can make it available to them.'

An old lecturer, as if awakened by the intoxication of what had been said, got up and declared: 'Today writers are all boring and one can't fathom why publishers have to go on printing them. I have read a few avant-garde books but they are all rubbish!'

A director of the publishing house hastened to intervene to pour oil on the waters: 'I cannot say anything on this question because it is not my specialist area. But let us remember that today adventures are no longer to be found in printed books as they were in the days of our childhood. Today they are to be found in finance, in the circulation of money, in the challenge of leasing, for example. Ideas come only where there is money at stake and one must exploit everything. And it is useless to put forward moralistic theories because business, if it is not exploitation, what is it?'

Even before the conference had ended the woman had left. In her office she found a message waiting for her from the student of literature, who wanted to see her for a very important reason.

They had a date in a bar but the student was anxious and went to meet her, passing through the pigeons in the cathedral square. A storm was about to burst — all the pigeons were agitated and making short and frequent flights, drifting haphazardly in the air. No sooner did he see the woman in the distance than the student ran to meet her showing her a bundle of pages and saying: 'I have written a novel about readers of books! An allegorical novel!'

He wanted to tell it to her at once standing there among the pigeons which were trying to flee from the gusts of wind. He said he was very pleased with his novel, which he had written in a spurt of fifteen days during which he had finally understood everything about books and readers of books. He was smoking one cigarette after another because of his excitement at having at last understood everything.

His novel began like this: There is a young literary critic who always has to take part in conferences of critics and writers — conferences with a lot of people who talk for days and days without ever stopping. One fine morning, waking up in a hotel where he is staying during one of these conferences, something really horrible happens to him.

The literary critic wakes up with a horror of words, of any words spoken or written by himself or others. He doesn't quite know what is happening to him but he feels a desire to be tied firmly to a bed with his mouth and ears sealed with sticking-plaster for some years, so as to able to submit in silence to the horror of the words that come out of his mouth and drive him out of his mind. Because he feels with certainty that when someone speaks it is never himself: that everything the words say has nothing to do with whoever utters or writes them, and that it arises only from the terrible obligation to say something to others all one's life long.

Naturally when he phones the management of the hotel to ask to be tied firmly to a bed, with his mouth and ears sealed with sticking-plaster for some years, no one understands his horror of words; and they take him for a madman and put him in a clinic.

Meanwhile in the cathedral square the pigeons, buffeted by the gusts of wind, take off in fits and starts, often collide and lose their feathers. The woman had set off at a good pace towards the arcade that opens to the square in search of a bar and the student pursued her anxious to tell her the rest of his novel.

In the rest of his novel the critic is in a clinic with a straitjacket, and they are giving him sedatives to make him sleep a long time. During that long sleep he has a long dream, which is the central part of the novel.

He dreams he is in a city right in the midst of an endless desert. Here he sees very clearly that the inhabitants are all bored to death, because to live in the midst of the desert and always to see sand dunes is rather boring. But the dreamer sees inhabitants in the street with a book in their hands, others reading sitting under a tree, others wandering over the desert paths as if they were plunged deep in a great stupor. After a little he sees what this state of stupor comes from: they are readers of books and are so deeply immersed in an infinite drugged state because of the books they have read, or the stories or the extremely boring words they have had to read in the books.

The dreamer sees too that these drugged people cannot detach themselves from books, because a state of amazement at the absolutely boring nature of the books has taken possession of them and they can no longer shake it off. But watching some of them, he realises that in that state of stupor there is also a kind of happiness. In fact, since the boring nature of the books is absolute, it absolves them of everything else and renders any other form of boredom irrelevant — including that of the desert which they have always before their eyes.

In the arcade that gives on to the square the woman and the student drank a coffee in a bar, while he continued to tell the story of his novel. Immediately afterwards the woman said she had to go back to her office. Meantime it has begun to rain and now the student is pursuing the woman through the rain to tell her the rest of his story.

At this point the story says that wandering about in the city in the desert, the dreamer meets many inhabitants dressed like Arab camel drivers going about with wagons full of books to sell to the drugged readers. These bogus Arab camel drivers organise caravans to cross the desert and each time they bring back tons of books, which they then try to dispose of either to the drugged people or to the rest of the population without making much distinction between the books they bring and the persons to whom they trade them. The drugged people do not notice anything, because all they want is to find the happiness of absolute boredom which mitigates the boredom of the desert.

However there are other inhabitants dressed like gangsters who protest against the merchants. They go about saying they can distinguish between good books and bad and do not let themselves be taken in by bogus camel drivers. They go about saying they know what is the Beautiful, the Good and the True, and never cease to present themselves to everyone as people who know how to pass judgment on these matters — therefore can pass judgment on anything — therefore can explain to everyone what they should do, say, think. Then these people who pass judgment on anything go on to annoy the drugged readers by criticising them for their stupid happiness and explaining to them what they should read.

In his dream the dreamer now finds himself at a conference of those same people dressed as gangsters and here he has the strange impression of being dead. But as a dead man at that conference he is unable to distinguish the bogus camel drivers from the bogus gangsters because they are all dressed like astronauts. He listens to an extremely long speech by an astronaut talking about books and writers and that speech feels so unbearable that suddenly he can no longer take it. He becomes upset and shouts 'Enough! Enough! This can't go on!' dead though he is. Thrashing about he wakes up in a hotel with a horror of words, of any words spoken or written by himself or others.

He wakes up in the same hotel where he woke up before with the same horrible sensation. While he is being taken back to the same clinic, with the same straitjacket, he at last understands what is happening to him: he understands that this cycle of horror at words and his internment in a clinic and the dream of a city in the desert must repeat itself to infinity until something comes to set him free.

In the cathedral square the pigeons were making flights more and more skewed and freakish: they no longer knew where to go in the rain and at this point the student wanted to know what the woman thought of his novel before taking it to a publisher. So he asked her: 'So what do you have to say about it? Remember that it is a vision, an allegorical novel like the ones they used to write once upon a time.'

The woman stopped in the rain and replied: 'I don't know how they used to write novels once upon a time. But if there is a God he is certainly not pleased that we have too many ideas about what goes on, or that we should listen to people who talk too much. I have listened to you enough — now go your own way and don't phone me any more.'

A couple of years later the ex-student of literature and the ex-young woman without a profession got married.

As a novelist he had not had any success — no publisher had agreed to publish his very odd novel. From then on he decided to change his life, finally to become another person. He tried many roads, he wandered through many cities, he crossed a couple of deserts encountering a certain number of dragons and monsters. Finally he returned to his own village and sat down on a chair seriously considering hanging himself. But he was held back by the thought that others would then have had to find him dead, that is to say in a somewhat depressing condition and one not particularly acceptable in circles that count.

One day he turned up at this ex-fellow lodger's, swearing that he had changed, that he really had become another person and saying he wanted to marry her. She listened to him for a whole day, saw that he hadn't changed at all, and agreed to marry him.

Thus ends the muddled youth of our ex-student of literature. Now he has become a literary critic like the character in his novel — he writes reviews for a mass-circulation weekly.

What he had learned in his first months of attendance at university — that is to say the way of being able to boast of having very thoroughly understood the books he has read — now has become his way through life.

He says in his profession the rule is more or less this: a person writes to boast of having understood something until someone takes him seriously and offers him a job. In order to be taken seriously, for a certain time he went in for dismissing an infinite number of things which simply did not appeal to him. He himself did not even know what he was doing, but someone took him seriously and now he has got a job.

He says that every so often great doubts come over him and he no longer knows if it is he or someone else who is writing and speaking. It is as if there were someone else about whom he knows everything, who lives with him and has to write something every week, pretending to know what he is talking about. Often he feels very lonely along with that other person.

Sometimes he is invited to take part in conferences of critics and writers with a lot of people who talk for days and days. But he doesn't go because he fears that the horror of words may well up in him and that he will enter a cycle of repetitions without an exit like the character in his novel. Fortunately the horror of words has not yet come to him, otherwise he would not be able to write his weekly reviews.

As well as writing reviews, every so often he has to do interviews, and today he interviewed an old writer who writes obscure books with little success. Now he is re-reading the interview, and some things said by the old writer puzzle him, give him a sense of danger.

He thinks it over: what will the readers who want clarity of ideas say about those words? And what will the other critics who have such clear ideas say?

Yes, but basically what is clear and what is obscure in words? They all seem so transparent but what are they vainly trying to say?

Since the other person who speaks and writes for us always wants to be safe, in order to keep him quiet one must always pretend to have fully understood what the words are trying in vain to say. Shame is the fire that devours these pretences but how the other person storms and stamps his feet to survive amid his convictions!

If only he could strike out, cancel, cause to disappear from the page those words of the old writer! That in itself would be a wonderful relief for the other person. Yet these words are there, they too having appeared in the vast world like rainworms in the earth.

Feeling very ashamed and definitely lost, the ex-student writes them below by way of a conclusion:

Everything that is written is already dust at the very moment it is written and it is right that it should be lost with all the other dusts and ashes of this world. Writing is a way of passing time, paying the homage that is due to it: it gives and takes and what it gives is only what it takes — so the sum is always zero, the insubstantial.

We wish only to be able to celebrate this insubstantial thing and the void, the shadow, the dry grass, the stones of crumbling walls and the dust we breathe.

THE DISAPPEARANCE
OF A PRAISEWORTHY MAN

I must have been about forty and aware that I was no longer young but a grown man with a linen jacket, crumpled and on the dirty side, something that went against my habits of cleanliness in my person and wardrobe. I kept seeing everyone looking round them to find their way in the park as if something had happened and they were looking for a way out, and I too was looking around me to get my bearings with the same futile gestures. My son was looking at a motorcycle illegally parked on the grass of the park with his mouth open to express his wonder at the chrome fittings of the object. Perhaps he was expecting me to share his wonder, or to add to it with something banal about motorcycles in general and about this model in particular; like a monkey he was also scratching his head with three fingers, as if they were a rake.

I thought that once I was young and now I was a grown man with a son who scratched his head when faced by the chrome fittings of a Yamaha bike only because the sun reflected its rays onto it, making it shine in an illusory manner. On the canal in the park a little barge passed with a noisy transistor and the thought came to me: Like a ship of the dead playing music. It was a Sunday morning and I noticed that there was nothing more to do, I am speaking for myself naturally, I don't give a damn about the others.

I had no sooner got home than I began to write this memoir,

asking myself what can have happened. It is as if God had changed the cards on the table without telling us anything. Otherwise why would this inane singer on the television shine with the halo of a demigod? Why should the chrome fittings of a Yamaha bike, barely touched by the rays of the sun, seem to point to thousands of earthly wonders? The substance of the desert mirages now glimmers everywhere.

I am straying from the point, as if slightly blind and no longer able to see clearly my goals as a man and a father — something which is certainly contrary to my principles. If I were then to show my son what I am writing I know he would not understand a thing; when I explain something to him he usually yawns.

The spot where I live is called Neuilly-sur-Seine and I am proud of it because of the 'Seine' included in its name, quite apart from the respectability of the place. Water I find restful; it always runs in the same way, always down and never up — I am talking about rivers naturally. And as I walk in the park on Sunday I look at it and say to myself: there — that's how the water goes — where to? I wouldn't be able to say on the spur of the moment.

Something must have happened one Sunday and it seems odd to me since Sunday is generally the day when nothing should happen. Walks in the park in the morning and television at home in the afternoon; in good weather the boats with Sunday people taking the sun in shorts and fantasy glasses; the gay and foolish youths on their roller-skates pass laughing through this void; the old distinguished couples turn to watch them with an astonished air simply to prevent themselves from falling down rigid with boredom and unreality etc. That is what Sunday is like in our parts, to put it concisely.

On Sunday I keep an eye on my son to see that nothing happens even in his simple life. Fortunately on other days he goes to school where I can be sure that nothing happens to him, nothing is imprinted on his mind, since he dozes all through his time in school and in the Metro as well both coming and going.

Education has always given him a certain somnolence — which is only natural given the lack of blows, tortures etc.

The school I have chosen for him bears a ridiculous American name, which seems to refer to some mystery or other connected with the business activities of men. In fact it is an institute where the students are precociously trained for a career in money, to worship money — as is the norm — to count it every morning and to predict ways of making it in large quantities. But for the time being my son is only studying meaningless numbers, is learning technical formulae by heart, sleeps and dozes and does nothing else. His life is as simple as his mind, and with this I am content.

Keeping an eye on him on Sunday so that nothing happens to him I have had the sensation for some time of looking at water — I have the feeling that he is like water which runs along because of uncontrollable circumstances, but without any real goal of its own. And I have often wondered how he will manage one day among financiers and businessmen in the arena where these gentlemen carry out their normal roles as butchers. The water runs away and they are like boulders which roll down from above, making it deviate into stagnant puddles, perhaps as a purifying sacrifice to the divinity of their deals.

That is all there is to be said for the moment. I fear I can already smell the smoke in which another useless life will end.

The firm for which I work deals in containers for liquid foods. In ten years it has become one of the biggest firms in the sector and I have become one of its directors although I have never seen a single one of the products we sell. We are middlemen, we deal with figures and letters, out of which we produce weekly reports and about which we talk with competence to the clients; the objects to which the letters refer are obscure things to us, but there are catalogues which speak clearly — and all the rest is so predictable!

Unknown voices on the telephone ask for information, I

consult the catalogues and reply with a certain courtesy. I invite strangers to lunch in a good restaurant and talk for hours about containers for liquid food which we are able to put at the disposal of the world — containers with a high degree of sterility and capable of preserving food in refrigerators for many months. Faced with so many figures and letters the strangers let themselves be persuaded — among other things because this is what they are seeking, to be persuaded of something, like all of us.

After which I send an invoice to our store in Lyons and that is how we make a career in our business, all of us being qualified persons as well as fathers of families. With what aim? For moral reasons, I suppose, children, the house etc.

A couple of times a year I have to go to Lyons to decide what supplies are necessary on the basis of the previsions of some astrologer concerning the number of yoghurts that will be consumed, the demand for preserved fruit, consommé, cream of mushroom or peas. Everything is so predictable, as I have said. I go through these storehouses examining the piles of boxes whose codes I recognise, but not their essence, and come back to Paris by night train, leafing through catalogues in six languages almost none of which I know.

Once they sent me to Switzerland to persuade some ordinary Swiss of the goodness of our containers, and there I at last saw something that seemed to me the opposite of our catalogues. Cows at pasture looked at me as if to say: 'Oh look, there's something out there in the world.' I saw from their glance that that was what they were thinking. They were thinking with surprise, 'Oh look, there's something out there,' thanks to the lack of catalogues. What did these cows see? Something indistinct and without a code, perhaps they saw the essence of the great void. That was why they had such a relaxed and relaxing air, I imagine.

When my work is done I leave the office in rue des Petits Carreaux and make my way through the people who throng the little fruit and vegetable market. Behind the orderly little piles of red apples, of yellow marrows, of carrot-coloured carrots you might think the sellers don't do badly — they still feel like cheerfully hailing people they don't know. Going down rue de Montorgeuil to get from the baker my four sticks of daily bread, sometimes I have a different impression: I have the impression that all of us in this busy street are the figures and letters in some catalogue, obscure matter of which no one knows the essence, although many sell it as familiar stuff. But yes, we are the signs and figures of this world, the reputation and pride of our administrators. That is a highly moral thought which came to me quite by chance.

Coming out at the church on the corner, St Eustache, I often turn my thoughts to God even if lately I have not been able to understand his will very clearly. Then there in front of the great square of Les Halles the great hole in the depths of the earth — and crowds of silly badly dressed young people some with T-shirts like trapeze artists, others with handkerchiefs round their foreheads, others in mourning, or else young blacks who play their tomtoms sitting on the steps at the entrance to the great hole.

Passing these young people without their noticing me, I often wonder: How is it possible that for them I am just anybody, one among the thousands of others who at this time are hurrying towards the Metro? Am I perhaps just anybody? Am I not something more whom they do not notice because of their heedlessness?

Certainly there is no doubt, I reply to myself. If nothing else then this memoir which I am writing in the language of my fathers could prove it: it is not something just anybody could write!

Entering the great hole I go down the escalators towards the Metro to return home with my sticks of daily bread and my little French-style moustache. And here sometimes I get the urge to buy a pornographic magazine which I shall then have to hide very carefully at home. What gives me the impetus is perhaps the idea that by examining the glance of these almost too naked women I may be able to understand their soul, to see the meaning of their codes.

I know that I am looking for a little excitement but only as a confused memory of love about which moreover I honestly know almost nothing. When my French wife was still alive I certainly did not imagine that we would bother about this sort of thing in bed — I had quite other things to think about in those days.

Since the Sunday when this thing that happened to me began, I wanted to be able to explore my son's mind so as to understand what effect the chrome fittings on that Yamaha bike had had on his poor brain. A son is like a mirror in which a parent sees himself and vice versa, provided naturally that the son doesn't merely yawn every time he has to speak to his father.

We had an appointment at midday near the office — I had invited my son to the restaurant, I don't remember why. Perhaps it is because I want to show myself to be good and generous towards the little youthful beast. I stopped at the corner of rue Réamur to watch him coming towards me in the distance, dragging the soles of his shoes with these overlong arms of his falling down to his thighs, with his clumsy air, his wandering glance. He seemed to have become too tall for his modest aspirations, he kept his shoulders bent so as not to stand out.

I still see him there, with his jeans held up by braces and that jersey with American slogans. Lately I have allowed him to wear jerseys with American slogans, hoping they may help him to learn English.

Lost among the crowd in the fruit and vegetable market, he was looking everywhere for me but I did not stand out. To me he seemed too lost, completely unaware of the goal towards which he was going. There, I said to myself, he is the water which is unaware of itself and goes along only because of the empty inertia of the ebb and flow.

I hurried away along the pavement and wanted to lose him, to separate myself from him because his goals were not mine, as I had that very moment perceived. Let us say that I cannot bear anyone who does not have a precise goal in life.

At a certain point I slowed down, saying to myself that he could not have seen me, that he is always half-asleep. I stopped and my son was drawing near, stretching his neck up above the crowd to look for me. I quickened my step in the opposite direction asking myself: What could I think of now that would not annoy me? What could I think of for the next twenty years with this son on my hands day after day?

Yes, of course, empty chatter. My son was still following me with his nose in the air to sniff out my path but without ever increasing his stride to catch up with me. I could have gone on walking for six days, walking from here to Normandy and back and he would still have followed me without ever quickening his pace, without ever a doubt, simply dragging the soles of his shoes along the streets. That is how water goes, I said to myself, now I know he is following the bed of a river but without direction; he cannot have a goal or aim in life.

An hour later we were seated in front of each other in a so-called self-service restaurant near the rue de Renard together with hundreds of other nobodies.

I recall with difficulty the essential threads of our conversation in the restaurant. At home we normally eat in silence, I read the paper, my son absorbs the food, his face in his plate; but here I felt the urge to keep the conversation alive, perhaps once again to show that I was nice and reasonable with the young animal.

First of all I tried to get him to understand how I would be able to unmask all the appearances and the illusory mirages which flash around us, including the reflections from the chrome fittings of the Yamaha bike. I am not easily enchanted by certain things. With my criticism I would be able to break down all the illusions that fill his skull, if I wanted to — did he understand this or not?

Absorbing a plate of lumpy spaghetti, my son replied innocently: 'Yes, yes, I understand.' I immediately dropped the subject out of decency; he hadn't understood a thing; of this I was certain.

Then I took up another topic of conversation. I asked him if he knew the story of Abraham and Isaac and how God had asked Abraham to sacrifice to him his son Isaac and how Abraham accepted this merely to please his god. To me it seemed a very cautious way of approaching a discussion of our necessary separation and in a fatherly way I attempted to make him reflect on it: 'It is a very instructive story about fathers and sons and about the tremendous sacrifices fathers have to face on account of their sons, don't you think, Leo?'

I suspect the young animal thought I was talking about a film on television. Otherwise his answer would be inexplicable: 'Is it a costume piece?' I explained to him nicely that we were talking about an event that took place some thousands of years ago. Swallowing his tinned fruit, my son replied: 'Yes, yes, but it's all boring stuff.'

With that I fell silent, overcome by his ignorance. That very evening in the Metro I was thinking furiously about the appropriate measures to get rid of him. Certainly the best and most traditional way is the knife — if I had raised a knife at him, at table for instance, he would have taken to his heels and fled from the house. But who could assure me that God would solve everything at the last moment as in the case of Abraham, and that I wouldn't be forced to cut off an ear at least?

To poison him would certainly have been easy from the domestic point of view. But then what did I know of the inscrutable wishes of God, who first asks us to be praiseworthy men, upholders of morality, and then leaves it to fathers to solve all the problems of life with some necessary murder in the family? I was unable to overcome my state of confusion in the deep darkness of paternal duty.

Thinking furiously I reached home. I ate supper alone and after supper I sat down in my study to make notes for this memoir. At that very moment of particular meditative effort my son came into the room and asked me vaguely: 'What are you writing, Poupi?'

Restraining my anger I said I was making notes about life in the language of my fathers. Stifling his laughter he asked: 'How many fathers did you have then?' I threw a wooden ornament at him, an object in indescribable taste acquired by my late wife, missing my target — his skull — but achieving another important result: that pathetic memory of my wife smashed into pieces and I could at last throw it into the rubbish.

Let us continue. How easy it is to describe a situation and then say: 'This is me.' A man quickly becomes the 'this' he indicates and until he dies will only indicate the 'this' he represents.

One night I woke with a start because of a brilliant idea that had come to me about how to get rid of my son. This is more or less what I thought: Certainly God does not claim from us real sacrifices — he is satisfied with some sort of spectacle or performance. He leaves us in the dark to smell the void that surrounds us, but he has become less demanding in the matter of sacrifices. Perhaps he wants us to be more civilised, less savage than his ancient patriarchs.

I pulled out of the cupboard an extremely old rigid fibre suitcase which I had not used for years. I put a label on it with the announcement: HERE IS A SUITCASE FOR YOU, MY SON, AND SOME MONEY. DO WHATEVER YOU WISH BUT LEAVE THE HOUSE. On tiptoe I went and placed it in front of my son's room so that he would see it clearly in the morning the moment he woke.

I went back to bed and fell asleep again pleased with the civilised solution I had found. Two days later the suitcase was still there, as far as I can see my dozy son had not noticed it.

During the evening meal I tried to drop hints about suitcases and journeys, to the number of enterprising young people who leave home to allow their parents to live in peace. My son looked at me with his mouth open unable to make anything of these hints. With a vague air he asked: 'Aren't you eating, Poupi?' I swallowed the mouthful I had in my throat and left the room without saying anything, out of a sense of decency.

That same evening I carried the fibre suitcase downstairs and left it beside a rubbish bin.

Yes, it must have happened on the same evening that I met on the stairs that stationmaster from Courbevoie, after leaving the suitcase in the street — almost desperate I might add. It was right there on the stairs that I met the stationmaster from Courbevoie.

It will be a good idea to say something about this man. He is a pensioned-off stationmaster who continues to wear his stationmaster's cap and takes upon himself to be concierge to the building. He lives in a cubbyhole on the ground floor with a precarious toilet arrangement on the landing. Sometimes, coming down the stairs, I hear him in his cubbyhole shouting and going on about his daughter who lives in Nogent married to a chemist, accusing her of brutishly leaving him to croak in that cubbyhole instead of taking him to live with her in Nogent.

Moreover he has the bad habit of interrogating me when I can't avoid him on the stairs. He wants to know: 'But are you really French?' and I say, 'Of Italian parents,' and he concludes, 'So not really French.' Once he came and rang my bell to ask me: 'Did you fight in the Resistance?' and on the spur of the moment I had to confess that I had not fought. He asked: 'But whose side were you on?' and I said: 'On nobody's side,' and he said: 'So you weren't on the side of the French.' I pointed out to him that at that time I was eight and living in another country and he went off muttering: 'I suspected that he wasn't French.'

Damned stationmaster from Courbevoie — I am always afraid of meeting him on the stairs, because I know that he would like to speak to me about his loneliness and sadness.

Now that evening the stationmaster was coming upstairs to tell me this: that the water tank for the radiators, situated goodness knows why in the attic above my flat, could not be emptied because the drainage pipe was blocked. Something that didn't matter a damn to me. But he said: 'There is a danger that when pumping water to clear the pipes the workmen may flood your house.'

Thinking himself to be concierge of the building, he busied himself with such eventualities and so was annoyed because he had come upstairs twice and twice had passed the news to my son, and my son had not said anything to me.

At that moment I felt a breath of solidarity swell my breast and I exclaimed: 'Children are useless — it would be better never to have had any.' This greatly cheered him, as I foresaw, giving him the chance of immediately having a go at his daughter who lives in Nogent along with his son-in-law, the greedy chemist.

He went on talking and I felt that he was happy, and I too was happy for him — happy at his imprecations and even at his blasphemy against God. When he then said in a serious voice: 'Children sap your strength and the more they grow the more they sap your strength, then leave us here like dogs without hope,' within myself I thought: Here at last is a man who understands me.

I was on the point of embracing him and inviting him in to discuss our problems as fathers. It would have been a nice evening, at last a little human understanding. But I confined myself to laying a hand on his shoulder in a gesture of fraternal friendship and he raised his stationmaster's cap as a sign of gratitude. I want back into the house and slightly relieved began to watch television.

It was Sunday. I was coming down avenue du Roule with my son on the way back from the park, and I saw these young people sitting on the chairs of an open-air bar dressed in black leather with studs everywhere. As we passed I heard them talking in that slang of theirs with its abbreviated words, a sure sign of laziness; I, for instance, never abbreviate any word, I drink their vanity to the dregs.

I was walking in a strange way, dragging my feet as if I were older than I am, I felt the weight of my son bearing me down. I saw him with these overlong arms of his falling on to his thighs, his hands which he never knows where to put and that stupid jersey with some slogan in American on it, the meaning of which he does not know.

Ungainly, my son. 'Stand up straight,' I used to say to him. 'Don't walk like an orangutan.' 'Yes, Poupi,' my son would reply. Often he calls me by that nickname — in his mind with a reference to my paternity but in his ignorance, without knowing it, using a name for a dog.

My son greeted the young people dressed in leather in the bar, raising his little hand in a pitiful way so as not to show me all his enthusiasm for this gang. And I saw myself with these ridiculous little French moustaches of mine, dragging myself along beside my son, asking myself: 'Why do these traffic lights, their immobility, weigh on me so — like the chairs and tables of this bar and the young people dressed in leather looking into space?' It seemed odd to me that in all that void there could be so much weight — not even a little of that feeling of lightness which, they say, astronauts find on the moon. Yet this was a desert like the moon. No liberty — I asked myself: 'Where?'

I felt that there was no use in stumbling along — I dashed off. The green traffic light, the cars shooting along the avenue, my corpulent son looking at me: 'Where are we going, Poupi?' a bovine voice. And I began to run between the cars which sounded and sounded their horns. I ran, hoping to drag that sheep of a son after me, saying to myself: 'Now the young animal is following me and he will be squashed flat by some mad motorist and so we will solve everything.' I did not turn round because I didn't want disappointments, I with my little moustaches and my principles.

In effect I felt as if I were soaring over the cars, I was in one of these rare moments when I see everything, control everything etc, etc.

Nothing. My son had stopped to look at a window full of electronic gadgets, he had not even noticed the efforts his father was making to resolve the family situation there in the midst of the traffic. I surprised him as, openmouthed, he contemplated these gadgets with the same blind wonder as he had contemplated the chrome fittings of the bike in the park. I said nothing — I cannot bear innocence, but I know that innocence is invincible if one confronts it head on.

I was walking smartly home, rue d'Armonville was completely deserted. My son came after me at a lazy pace.

After this failed resolution of my family problems it was before lunch that I caught my son in the act once more. Entering his room I asked him: 'What is that suitcase?' 'I found it.' I noticed an extremely old rigid fibre suitcase beside his bed, an indecent suitcase and certainly not very clean.

'Found it where?' I asked. My son made vague gestures as he explained: 'On the sidewalk. Someone must have moved house and thrown it away.' I say: 'Don't gesticulate — one talks with one's mouth not with one's hands.' He says: 'Yes, Poupi.'

At the door I turned round and gave my son the order: 'Take that suitcase down right away, don't make a fuss with it, and leave it in the street. I don't want to see it any more.' But my son was contemplating the suitcase: 'I can't — there are records in it.' I threw him a stern fatherly glance: 'Did you steal them?' My son looked out of the window as if he were talking to someone else: 'I swopped various things.'

Naturally I could not believe this stupid invention. I went up to him so as to pinch his arm: 'Leo, watch what you are doing, eh?' Then in a low voice: 'If you steal I shall let you go to prison, understood?' My son looked out of the window rubbing his pinched arm: 'All right, Poupi, don't worry.'

Then I too looked out of the window, and at that moment I saw the world going past under a street lamp; but I was too tired to believe my eyes.

That afternoon various things happened and too many of them for my liking. The sun was still shining on the lawn of the hospice for old people opposite my house when someone rang the doorbell. It was that Armenian called Gérard — someone who thinks he is my colleague only because our offices communicate and no well-closed door divides them. I thought for a moment: If he is Armenian how come that he is called Gérard? I did not remember his surname.

Keeping the door half-shut I asked, 'What do you want?' so that he wouldn't get it into his head to enter my home when he felt like it. 'I have to talk to you,' said the Armenian. I noticed that his accent was not perfect like mine, although I am as much of a foreigner as he is in this country. But one needs years and years of self-correction to have a good accent, neither frivolous nor popular, and not everyone is prepared to correct themselves.

'I have no time,' I said to him and was going to shut the door. Then when Gérard spoke I understood that he was inviting me home to have a drink — he lives near me. I replied vaguely: 'At six,' and shut the door.

My son passed by scratching his stomach, 'Who was it, Poupi?' he asked. I aimed a kick at his groin but he dodged. 'I don't want you to call me Poupi,' I told him, 'You have to call me father.'

My son couldn't help laughing when he heard that word — I saw him scratching his stomach and wanting to laugh, 'Repeat it — "father",' I ordered him. 'Father,' my son repeated. 'Now repeat — "Who was it, father?"' 'Who was it father?' he repeated. 'None of your business, you little bastard,' I answered more or less.

I thought that in this way I had dealt with some matters outstanding and that I could at last sit down to watch a normal television programme. But suddenly something else happened which I still cannot understand. While my son was urinating in the toilet I went in like a fury and shouted at him, gesticulating:

'I feel free, do you understand?' He continued to urinate, replying without looking at me: 'Yes, Poupi.'

I stood there wondering what we had been trying to say to each other, I with these words and he with that answer. I stood there without moving in the door of the toilet while I heard my son in his bedroom putting on the usual record — a black woman's voice which repeats an infinite number of times the same words, melancholy words, silly words, which he in any case doesn't understand — I found this out by questioning him.

I set out for Gérard's when it was already dark, I wanted to have some distraction. I walked as far as Porte Maillot to try to understand who I was, not as a distraction. As it happened I had scarcely come out of the rue d'Armenonville than I met two tall prostitutes with black patent leather boots and short lamé skirts, like two warriors; they were followed by a black with a checked cap exactly like mine. It seemed to me to be a sign that the stars were about to announce something fishy even in our respectable district.

I must take care that my memoir does not become a farce, I was thinking one day. Apart from everything else because for some time now all the words sound so false that no one can any longer believe another man any more unless he talks in numbers and symbols. Ah yes, I have noticed. There came to my mind those shopkeepers in rue Rambuteau, who have such faith in their cheese, their salads, herring and sauces, but when they look at you you see that they simply cannot believe in your spiritual existence.

I was in my office, sitting motionless looking at the window and pondering. Outside it was raining and I thought: If it rains at least let me see the clouds. I moved my chair in front of the window to look at the clouds, but the low gutter covered the whole sky and there facing me were only other windows of other offices. A man with whiskers in the French style like mine made signs of greeting from one of the windows. I said to myself: Who does that man think he is casting a spell on with his gestures of greeting? I do not know him and I do not want to know him.

But the man who was greeting me was so like me in his dress, in the cut of his hair, in his general attitude of an office animal, that I had the strong suspicion that it might very well be he who was writing my memoir, or at least a memoir similar in all ways, based on the script that unites us and makes us so alike.

As numerous as the stars are lives identical one with the other, interchangeable, and who can tell me that the privilege of some spiritual difference is not also a mirage of the desert? It might be that all that I have seen, felt, suffered, is only the painful confession of that man who is greeting me.

Anxious to find out something, I at once called my secretary, the no longer young Madame Agnès, and I asked her if I was really identical with the man in the office opposite. I remember that Mme Agnès gave a benevolent smile and assured me: 'Oh no, you are more distinguished.' I don't know why the impulse came over me to put my arm round her waist and say to her: 'Madame Agnès, would you give me a kiss?'

She took off her glasses to think about it and then she reflected: 'But my husband is through there,' (he's an employee of our firm) and I answered: 'Oh don't worry, he only thinks about outings with his friends and his sailing boat and nothing else — it's all foreseen.'

Yes, because I see myself in a story — I have it all in my head and know that here everything is already arranged and foreseen. I see this story in which I find myself, I see the people in the street and I know that they all move according to an arranged script. And in that same mysterious script everything a man will encounter is foreseen, written in an improbable memoir; it is like being in another person's dream.

That day or some other day — it is not important — I came home at an unusual time. I put the key in the lock, opened the door and there — it was no dream — the whole house was flooded, the water was running down the walls, my wife's wretched ornaments were sailing towards the sitting room and now that the door was open the flood was running out towards the stairs. Splashing about with a certain satisfaction, I watched the water run away.

Certainly this too was foreseen as if I had always known it — the water tank for the radiators, situated over my flat, having been pumped too full to unblock a pipe, was now spilling into my apartment — about a ton of it.

When a panting plumber came running up to tell me: 'Disaster,' I replied calmly: 'I knew it already.' I already knew that it was all the fault of my son whom the plumber had asked to shut off the water with the appropriate tool, but he had completely forgotten, being entirely lost in his youthful drowsy state. To the plumber I repeated calmly: 'I knew already that it was going to end like this.'

Now my son was in school, the water was running down the stairs to the first floor and seeping into the stationmaster's cubbyhole through a little skylight. And indeed who else would the water have been able to go and disturb? This too I knew already as I knew that if I went downstairs I would hear the laments and blasphemous curses of the stationmaster.

So I didn't bother too much about all this. Without bothering about anything I went into my flat to get a pair of dark glasses, put them on and made my way down the stairs to go for a walk. Indeed I also put on my checked cap — one never knows.

When I reached the ground floor I heard the laments of the stationmaster addressed to his daughter who lives in Nogent but also in particular to his son-in-law, the chemist. He was saying more or less: 'You scoundrel who have taken away my daughter and keep her to help you in the chemist's shop not because you love her — you are a heartless businessman. Scoundrel, and I have to live in this mousehole that's now flooded. What did I work fifty years for, scoundrel? Look here I have water in my shoes whilst you are dry.'

He was lamenting as foreseen only to say: 'I am a man, ecce homo, that's me, that's me!' But there are so many 'me's' about in this world, the sidewalks are full of them. Passing in front of him I greeted him with a quick touch of my cap and went out into the open air.

In cafés reading the paper — this is something new — I had never done it before. Why does one read a newspaper? To notice something without finding out anything more, knowing that it will always be the same old stuff and letting the words, the sentences and the pages go by like the days — all the same.

One afternoon I read a memoir, I must have been sitting in the gardens of the Tuileries and it was a very boring read. I admired the man who had written it. It must be great, I said, to be able to be so boring. So boring that everyone leaves you because they find nothing to discover in you, no anticipation of unexpected happenings, they look at you like a shoe, a stone or a tree etc.

These are loose speculations which lasted some days after the flooding of the house. I slept away from home, I ate away from home, no news of my son — there was a feeling of spring about.

In short, one evening I slept in my office feeling free and the morning after I ran down the stairs feeling lost. I am lost, I am lost, I thought. I asked myself if this too was foreseen and what it meant. I saw that in that word there was a mystery — lost for whom? lost for what?

In the street I wanted to find out if that word could be applied to other people too. If it is applicable to others too it is not serious, I reflected. And so a little optimism returned because if I had been able to check things a bit perhaps all this story in which I find myself would have turned out to be an illusion, another mirage of the desert.

On the boulevard Sébastopol the newspaper stall was shut — it seemed a bad sign to me. A bad sign too the newspaper poster hanging on the stall — a piece of paper washed out by the rain.

And on the boulevard there was no one except a tramp sitting on the steps of a shop — one of the kind who sleep on the ground in the square of the Beaubourg — and he watched me from afar.

A black crossed at the traffic lights with a specially light step, and I at once identified him as someone who does not feel lost.

The cafés on the boulevard were shut and then I remembered that it was a holiday. That was the explanation of all this emptiness! So long as there is an explanation one can manage to invent we are still safe. But perhaps hereabouts no one was lost — I would have to go and look elsewhere.

Twice I crossed the boulevard going towards Les Halles with a kind of desire to challenge the cars which passed undisturbed. If a car had run me down that would have been a fact not another stupid illusion. That would be a sure way of checking things, I said to myself.

The car with yellow lights had stopped sharply in front of me. The driver was looking at the shop windows casually while I was crossing the street by the pedestrian crossing. This too is a fact, I thought, he did not run into me and moreover he is looking at the shop windows casually.

Taking a long way round I came out into the rue du Temple and now it was as if I wanted to show everybody that I was just walking about without any valid reason. The others too were walking about without any valid reason, this I understood, but yet without giving visible signs of being lost.

How can one retell the wanderings of someone who in strict logic should not be me, given my principles, but whichever way one looks at it I don't see who else it could be? Day after day I went all over the city on foot, by bus, by Metro, doing my research.

On a fine sunny morning I was in the park of the Buttes Chaumont, watching the mothers taking a walk with their children, the young couples lying on the grass, the man who sells candy floss on the pathway, and all the rest without valid motives. Up there on a rocky peak in the middle of the lake someone was watching me through a telescope, I think; and then I asked myself if they might perhaps have identified me as a lost man, since I was by now so easily recognisable.

Yes, because at least things would be clear, everyone would have his turn to cast a rejecting glance at me, a mournful glance, as people do to persons who are lost or destroyed, however one cares to put it. And I would have something interesting to say about my excursions because of these glances.

A sinister light would accompany me as a signal of danger to anyone who wants to be happy while I go along the boulevard Haussmann among crowds of shoppers coming out of the supermarket, or emerge into the boulevard des Capucines to carry on my researches. There, mixed up with the extremely respectable people who throng the pavement in front of the open air cafés, I could also — if I so wished — take on the appearance of an assassin while I look and look. Look at what? I look at everything but see everywhere only that unending script.

One evening I got lost near the place Blanche under a dark sky; I was trying to see where all that wind was coming from that battered me; I suspected that it came from the central glacier of God the Almighty Father, but who can say with certainty? I was among so many other bit-players of life — one imitating a singer, another an author, another a government minister, another some woman or other; I was there with my little moustache in the French style.

In the square, coaches of tourists were emptying for a rapid visit to the celebrated pleasure spots. Brutish tramps brushed against me as they passed, asked me for a cigarette, and I could not even start up a healthy conversation since I do not have the vice of smoking.

Oh great city, useless steps, oh ways through the foreseen infinity! One morning I came out of the miserable hotel where I was staying and by mistake was almost about to go to work. At the last moment I decided to interrogate my lust and soon after I went up the rue Saint Denis looking at the women for sale, with skirts and without skirts, in the early morning doorways. I remember their frank gestures, the frank voices with which they stated the sum fixed to be allowed to penetrate their bodies. Sailors, commercial travellers, shopkeepers, who exchanged witty repartees, cats, peepshow signs. Not even this piece of research gave a result; all that frankness was for me an insurmountable obstacle, like innocence.

Being lost, we expect that others will find us, because only they can find us in all the universe. That's so, but our little flickering light cannot be brought to life again with too much frankness; there is always its useless secret that has to be respected.

One evening I was looking at the water in the Vallette basin — there in the wide space beyond the gate of the St Denis canal lock, the memory of ancient barges lost among the clouds. The sky was full of water and luminous worms, which shone and shone up there. No other sign.

One day after another like that. And one late afternoon I found myself near my house opposite Porte Maillot. Everywhere I saw crowds of me's going about in the streets, and they were lost streaming as far down as the place de l'Etoile and to the right up to the skyscrapers of the Défense. Thousands and thousands of me's, all the same, who had nothing to do with one another. They all wandered about like flickering lights shot through with shivers, always because of the wind which perhaps comes from the central glacier of God the Father; they wandered in the rain, standing there at the traffic lights, as numerous as the stars, right down to the Trocadéro and Auteuil and down to the river.

I said to myself: take a good look at them, they go on and on as foreseen by the clocks, some on foot, some in cars, some by other means; they hurry on towards the shopping streets or towards the amusement streets or towards the streets where they will at last be able to sleep; they crowd the streets, the squares, the side streets, they walk along always shot through by shivers; but they do not expect anything, and above all they do not for a moment think they are lost. They are like that — like water and dust — they wander about and work, wander about and buy things, wander about and sleep. To sleep and sleep — that is what is important.

I remember I went down into the Metro one Sunday and later found myself in the rue des Petits Carreaux, where my office is, looking at the door I go into every morning. I think I pressed the button to open the little entrance door and saw that I was about to go up; habit guided me — that is what makes the world go round. Someone passed me, greeting me confidently: 'How are things?' I did not reply — it was raining.

Walking in the rain — perhaps I was in Etienne Marcel — I began to turn over thoughts I had never had before, which do not belong to me and which I therefore do not recognise as mine. I do not remember them either, I try to imagine them, perhaps I invent it all. It doesn't matter — let us confuse the suffocating thought — let being without hope at least bring us to this point and that without feelings of remorse.

An evening walk, I am talking about an evening walk and I get shivers down my back. Where exactly has God gone and hidden himself? What am I doing in the world with this moustache and this checked cap? Why do I walk and breathe and feel time run away?

Who knows how I ended up in the square des Innocents, always innocence in my path. Perhaps innocence is a demon which everyone aims to trap, dedicating to it sanctuaries for the sale of immensely stupid things, objects that gleam, coloured objects; but when they have entrapped it what will happen? These are my reflections.

In the square des Innocents I saw a Honda 750 parked near the fountain. I recognised it and noticed that I can recognise all the makes of motorcycle if I feel like it. In a puddle I saw the neon gleam of the fast-food place in the square; I could understood all the gestures of the persons in the place, of the ones who came out with a sandwich in their hands, or eating chips, or drinking Coca-Cola. I was not a stranger to anything that surrounded me, I knew the habits of this world to perfection.

I saw myself thus for a moment — I too am expert in the customs of this world, capable of talking about them and explaining them and even of justifying them as 'a historical mutation'. It is a possibility, I said to myself, but I am another person, let's get that into our heads.

The desire arose in me to mix with the crowd, I went down into the Metro again. And down there I had the desire to follow the movements of people — the groups of boys and girls who come to Paris on a Sunday to go to the movies, and then to be that uncouth youth who was exploding crackers, the one who was teasing an old woman, the one who was making a speech to the people. I liked being in Les Halles, there in the depths of the earth, among the multitude, and to be dragged out from the crowd by a pack of wolves or a herd of calves perhaps; and then to listen to the confused youths of the boulevard Sébastopol who talked in half words, without sentences, and sent to the devil a proud man full of sentences, one who resembled me exactly.

As I went through the square again I liked those in the bars who talked loudly, screaming like ill-mannered people. I watched them with fascination always contradicting, contradicting everyone, without a care for anyone. Two cops passed and there rose up in me a love for all the policemen in the world: It is marvellous! I said to myself, they are the lowest of the low, they know it, and without false modesty they go about with heads held high. I too would like to be like that.

In the square a little handcart full of old furniture pulled by three girls with long hair and old rags that hung around them — they too bit-players of life, imitating poor mendicants. And I had the desire to follow the girls, to corner them one by one in the shadows of rue St Martin, to become the sex monster who assaults young girls, making grimaces, strangling etc.

On the quai of the Hôtel de Ville in the distance the lamps had a reddish halo, but from under the diffused light there spread cold colour from blue to indigo. The cars came at high speed towards the bridge and all of them seemed to have a precise goal; far off one heard the two-note call of an ambulance and on the pavement no one was surprised; I saw a woman raise an arm and a taxi stopped right in front of her; two boys ran across the street and one lost a shoe.

Under the trees of the quai someone said in the shadow: 'Where did you hear that story?' Further on an old woman commented vigorously: 'It's true!' A kind of hippy in a striped jersey was saying to another: 'I live at Noisy-le-Sec.' In a bar someone was making conversation and I thought: 'It's working — it is a fine conversation.' There arose in me a great sympathy for those who were talking at the nearby table, they were careful and clever with words.

I had the impression that one of my cheeks was crumbling through age and the force of gravity. I would have liked to speak to someone about how to grow old. I left the bar, it was late.

Like a dog on the lead I was brought back home by a double of myself with a little French moustache. For all that I know the distant stars and the rotating rings of the nebulae and the globes produced by the aggregation of matter, all this continued in the same way and with the same results; but for me as I entered rue d'Armenonville again all this was already reduced to a handful of appearances which put this one question to me: 'Who are you?' The rest is always very easily foreseen.

In the house there were big patches of damp everywhere and some little puddles due to the flooding. Something that didn't matter a fig to me, and didn't matter either to my son as far as I could judge. After supper I went back to thinking over what had happened, starting from that Sunday of revelations, with before me these notes which I am taking so as not to allow myself to be surprised.

I once more saw my son in the park scratching his head like a monkey, looking at the reflections of the sun on the chrome of the Yamaha bike. I saw from his gestures and from the way he opened his eyes wide that he had been struck by a great passion and I would never be able to save him. Something outside of him had shaken him and when I noticed it it was already too late; his demon had already been entrapped by appearances and my son scratched and scratched in astonishment.

After about an hour of reflection I said to myself: If my son should dress up with studs, put on women's earrings, or become a building contractor what does that change? Everything is so foreseeable. Now I too am exposed to things and soon I shall realise that I am part of the appearances like everyone else; then, re-reading these notes I shall perhaps take myself for a mediocre comedian who, along with his son, repeats the same gags to infinity.

Then I murmured to myself: 'I already see my fate. But at least for this bloody evening I am still myself until proof to the contrary.' I abandoned my notes and went into my son's room to see what he was doing, to question him about the effect the chrome fittings had had on his poor brain.

My son was doing nothing, he was lying on the bed with his fat body that is too big for his age, naked except for his pants. He was lookng at the ceiling and listening to the infinite monotony of that music, to that black woman who always repeats the same phrases, melancholy phrases, one doesn't know for whom. I asked him point blank; 'What are you doing?' and he sat up in bed and looked at me without answering.

I went to take off the tape, a little cassette in a recorder, and tried to break it, pressing on the edges with my thumbs. We looked into each other's eyes fleetingly like father and son, that is to say in the usual surly way; but he did not react, he was thinking about something else.

I did not manage to break the tape, it merely got twisted. I saw myself there in my vest making useless efforts to tear a little plastic object and who knows why. I was acting as if I were blind and no longer saw any goal in my life as man and father.

Leaving the room I heard my son yawn noisily behind me, indifferent to everything, incomprehensibly serene. Perhaps he lives in dreams; I don't, as a father and praiseworthy man, I have always detested dreams.

But now as I left that room it was as if I was going far off, far away from the son whose face I had already forgotten. As for me I don't know what my face was like; certainly I still had my moustache but as for the rest very little was predictable.

I slipped into bed smoking a cigarette in the dark; it is conducive to sleep. My thoughts went to my dead parents, Italians who had come to this country to make their fortunes, whom the young animal never knew because I didn't want him to know them, because I didn't want him to know from what a lineage of suffering, almost wild animals, he was descended through me. Among other things they spoke very bad French and that always seemed to me a good reason for not letting him know them.

My parents sleep in an Italian cemetery near the sea in Calabria, close to a very expensive tourist restaurant. Before falling asleep I tried to imagine what prices they charged in that restaurant for a full meal.

When one has begun something one must go on, like footsteps which come one after the other, like the lamp posts which come one after the other without ever stopping. Do we perhaps stop to count the lamp posts as we walk along? It would be absurd, one must continue, continue.

And so this man goes on towards an opaque future after writing the memoir we have just read. He continues every day in the office looking at the window for hours and signing invoices which his office secretary — the no longer young Madame Agnès — brings every moment, because of the noticeable increase in the volume of business in his firm.

But the day will come when this man will say to Madame Agnès: 'I can't sign this because I no longer am me, I am another person.' And to confirm the accuracy of his words, he will lean forward to kiss her on the lips whispering: 'I'm no longer me, believe me. I want someone to listen to me and I beg for your understanding.'

Madame Agnès will benevolently agree to listen to him and then this man will talk about a thousand different things in an inconclusive way — about the water which runs away and then evaporates into the universe, about fathers and sons, and also about the Swiss cows which had once looked at him with the air of saying: 'Oh, there's something out there in the world.'

Then the same man will feel pressed to leave the office before it is time for it to close, and he will go downstairs carried by an impulse which will point like a compass towards his obscure celestial pole. At home he will fill an old rigid fibre suitcase, found in the street by his son, with a few clothes, and he will put on his son's walkman and listen to the incomprehensible voice of a black woman who sings, monotonously, always the same words.

Then suddenly he will see himself in an unknown place, finally feeling himself for some reason like other people, and like the others on the road to an unknown future of innocence.

A few hours later he will leave home with a checked cap, knickerbockers, dark glasses, French-style moustaches, a walkman on his head. In a taxi he will go and pick up Madame Agnès, who meantime has become blonde, because of a very beautiful wig, and all dressed in pink with big patent leather boots like a warrior.

The two will have themselves taken by taxi to the airport, certainly now a little changed in their looks and indeed un-recognisable when they get into the plane, if only because of their happy expressions of expectant tourists.

In the last picture anyone will have of them they will be on a great plain among the mountains, both in climber's clothes with climber's sticks, about to set off for the snow-covered mountains in the distance. They will walk at a good pace and always with happy expectation — to go where? Where? But who can say where a man is going? Often one thinks he knows but it is a mistake.

All that one knows is that one must go on, go on, go on like a pilgrim of this world, until the awakening, if the awakening ever should come.